PLUNKITT
of
TAMMANY HALL

A SERIES OF VERY PLAIN TALKS ON VERY
PRACTICAL POLITICS, DELIVERED BY
EX-SENATOR GEORGE WASHINGTON PLUNKITT,
THE TAMMANY PHILOSOPHER,
FROM HIS ROSTRUM—
THE NEW YORK COUNTY COURT HOUSE
BOOTBLACK STAND

Recorded by
William L. Riordon

With an Introduction by
Peter Quinn

SIGNET CLASSICS

SIGNET CLASSICS
Published by New American Library, a division of
Penguin Group (USA) Inc., 375 Hudson Street,
New York, New York 10014, USA
Penguin Group (Canada), 90 Eglinton Avenue East, Suite 700, Toronto,
Ontario M4P 2Y3, Canada (a division of Pearson Penguin Canada Inc.)
Penguin Books Ltd., 80 Strand, London WC2R 0RL, England
Penguin Ireland, 25 St. Stephen's Green, Dublin 2,
Ireland (a division of Penguin Books Ltd.)
Penguin Group (Australia), 250 Camberwell Road, Camberwell, Victoria 3124,
Australia (a division of Pearson Australia Group Pty. Ltd.)
Penguin Books India Pvt. Ltd., 11 Community Centre, Panchsheel Park,
New Delhi - 110 017, India
Penguin Group (NZ), cnr Airborne and Rosedale Roads, Albany,
Auckland 1310, New Zealand (a division of Pearson New Zealand Ltd.)
Penguin Books (South Africa) (Pty.) Ltd., 24 Sturdee Avenue,
Rosebank, Johannesburg 2196, South Africa

Penguin Books Ltd., Registered Offices:
80 Strand, London WC2R 0RL, England

Published by Signet Classics, an imprint of New American Library, a division
of Penguin Group (USA) Inc. Previously published in Dutton and Meridian
editions.

First Signet Classics Printing, November 1995
20   19   18   17   16   15   14

Introduction copyright © Peter Quinn, 1995
All rights reserved

THE WORLD OF PRACTICAL POLITICS ACCORDING TO PLUNKITT

—There is a vital difference between "honest" and "dishonest" graft.

—It is important to be loyal to your friends—even up to the penitentiary door.

—For a politician, reading and other forms of education can have harmful effects.

—Patronage should be honored as the supreme form of patriotism.

—Never forget the importance of perfecting the gentle art of strong-arming votes . . . and everything else you never learned in high school civics class, as revealed by the man who wanted his epitaph to be "He Seen His Opportunities, and He Took 'Em."

PLUNKITT OF TAMMANY HALL
A Series of Very Plain Talks on Very Practical Politics

George Washington Plunkitt was born into poverty in New York in 1842. He had only three years of formal schooling, but this did not hinder him from becoming one of the most powerful men in New York City politics. He died in 1924, a renowned civic leader and a millionaire.

William L. Riordon, a newspaperman for the *New York Evening Post,* interviewed George Washington Plunkitt and preserved his philosophy for posterity. He recognized in Plunkitt an exceptional frankness that set him apart from his fellow bosses. In *Plunkitt of Tammany Hall,* Riordon admits readers into an area of life that mystified middle-class Americans at the turn of the twentieth century.

Peter Quinn is a former speechwriter for Mario Cuomo and the author of *Banished Children of Eve: A Novel of Civil War New York.*

Ex-Senator George Washington Plunkitt, on his rostrum,
the New York County Court House Bootblack Stand
(Copy of the original frontispiece in the first edition of 1905)

CONTENTS

INTRODUCTION

"OF ALL our passions and appetites," wrote Edward Gibbon, the famed chronicler of Rome's decline and fall, "the love of power is the most imperious and unsociable nature, since the pride of one man requires the submission of the multitude." It is a mystery what Gibbon would have made of George Washington Plunkitt, leader of the Fifteenth Assembly District, Sachem of the Tammany Society, holder of assorted public offices (at one point four simultaneously), a man skilled at seeking power yet who shunned all imperiousness and proclaimed sociability as the first law of politics.

For his part, it seems fairly certain that Plunkitt neither knew nor had any desire to learn about Gibbon's theories on leadership or the role it played in the fate of Imperial Rome. Had they been contemporaries and neighbors, Plunkitt might well have spent an afternoon conversing with Gibbon, though if this small book is any guide, Plunkitt was more given to soliloquies than conversations. But there's no doubt that as disinterested as Plunkitt might have been in Roman history, he would have paid careful attention to the needs and concerns of a constituent. *And what brings ya here, Mr. Gibbon? Is it a job you're seekin'? Or is that boy of yours in trouble again? Not to worry, Mr. Gibbon, you've come to the right place.*

This collection of short disquisitions or lectures or rambling observations—in truth, a mixture of all three—is a unique document. Aside from a few newspaper interviews and the official transcripts of numerous investigatory bodies, it is our only written record of the thoughts, musings and philosophy of the men who operated the most successful and long-running urban political machine in American history.

The dislike of the Tammany leadership for public statements or speeches is legendary. It was raised to an art form by its greatest tactician and most taciturn chief, Charles Francis Murphy, whose longest written statement is, perhaps, the four-sentence tribute that he composed (or more likely, commissioned) for Plunkitt's book. So famous was Murphy for his silences that when an observer once commented on the fact that the Boss was standing with his mouth shut during the singing of the national anthem, a Tammany brave replied that the Boss wasn't being unpatriotic. He just didn't want to commit himself in public.

There is no question that as well as being a unique American political document, Plunkitt's book is also among the most lively. This is the text free of convoluted theorizing, or impenetrable statistical analyses, or the mind-numbing language of the social sciences. It is politically incorrect in every sense, displaying equal contempt for "good government" reforms and for the conservative proponents of free enterprise as a solution for every social problem. "It's a grand idea," says Plunkitt, "the city ownin' the railroads, the gas works and all that. Just see how many thousands of new places there would be for the workers in Tammany!" Plunkitt makes little or no attempt to censor himself, even when it comes to offensive and despicable racial and ethnic epithets.

Plunkitt's formal schooling lasted, as he tells us, "three winters when I was a boy." In spite of (or more likely, because of) this, he is forceful and concise in expression and has a keen appreciation of the power of anecdote. Whatever readers might think of Plunkitt's opinions on the Civil Service or on the propriety of politicians wearing formal dress clothes, they will be hard put to forget the story of the young man driven by frustration with the Civil Service to fight with the Spanish at the battle of San Juan Hill, or of the young politico reduced by his love of formal wear to a hobo. Spun out a little longer, these are New York yarns worthy of O. Henry.

The pungent wit and concise effectiveness of each of Plunkitt's "plain talks on very practical politics" raise a question that isn't often asked but should be: How much is Plunkitt? And how much William L. Riordon, the newspaperman who listened to Plunkitt hold forth from his rostrum—the New York County Court House bootblack stand—and wrote it all down? Anyone who has transcribed an interview or conversation and then shaped it into readable prose knows the dimensions of the challenge. Often enough, the editor must do so much cutting, reorganizing and filling in, he deserves status as coauthor of the piece.

What's more, there is an amazing affinity between the flesh-and-blood Plunkitt and the fictional Martin J. Dooley, the contemporaneous Chicago barkeep and nonpareil American political philosopher invented by another Irish-American newspaperman, Finley Peter Dunne. Like Plunkitt, Mr. Dooley went about armed with the sharp, bitter shiv of the Irish comic sensibility, an attitude so attuned to the presence of absurdity in human affairs that it finds it hard to take anything seriously. Here, for example, is Mr. Dooley on reformers, words that if delivered in New Yorkese might as easily have come from Plunkitt: "A man that'd expict to thrain lobsters to fly in a year is called a loonytic; but a man that thinks men can be tu-rrned into angels by an iliction is called a rayformer an' remains at large."

Though we will never know with certainty where Plunkitt ends and Riordon begins, it seems safe to say that whatever editing he did, Riordon captured the authentic man, wit and wisdom, warts and all. Along with being richly larded with stories and anecdotes, these talks reek of a real-life professional utterly free of the grating tendency of modern-day politicians to apologize for taking up their trade.

Today, in our confessional age, it is common for those who enter politics to claim they are driven by a psycho-neurotic impulse "to give something back" to the system. Once in office, elected officials as well as appointed ones begin plotting their eventual departure, paying careful and solicitous attention to the industry or business that will one day find their experience and connections attractive. With this lucrative prospect in mind, they regulate or legislate for the very firms or corporations they hope to be employed by. The game is wrapped inside the techno-jargon that the financial and service industries are so adept at creating, but it still comes down to the formula of George Washington Plunkitt: "I seen my opportunities, and I took 'em."

Plunkitt is compellingly honest about the true lure of politics—first and foremost, the desire to hold and wield power—and about the rewards those who take up such a calling might expect. According to Plunkitt, "when a man works in politics, he should get something out of it." In another place, Plunkitt defines that something as "honest graft," an oxymoron that has come to summarize for many the venality at the heart of Tammany.

Greed there was aplenty throughout the history of Tammany. It is estimated that William Magear Tweed and his Ring stole in the vicinity of $50 million (multiply by ten to get today's equivalent) before they were caught. Boss Croker, an immigrant boy who apprenticed with the Fourth Avenue Tunnel Gang and at an early point in his political career was tried for murder, made no secret that he was working for his own pocket "all the time." In conjunction with Police Chief Bill Devery, Big Tim Sullivan, a friend of Plunkitt's and district leader of the lower East Side, ran a multimillion-dollar gambling syndicate. Plunkitt's obituary in the *Times* of November 23, 1924, estimates that "the Senator's estate will amount to considerably more than $1,000,000." Seven years after Plunkitt's death, in 1931, the inquiry led by Judge Samuel Seabury brought to light the magical tin box of Sheriff Farley and the massive peculations it was symbolic of, an exposé that forced the resignation of Mayor Jimmy Walker.

A detailed accounting of the thievery connected with Tammany would run to volumes. But while the plundering was often fearsome, it would be a mistake to imagine that Tammany enjoyed a corner on the corruption market, or that the long reign of the Organization was little more than a succession of comico-criminal Irish pols who had no concept of what to do with the power they held other than to line their pockets and employ their friends.

In America, bribery and influence peddling have always been bipartisan affairs, and Tammany's appetite for ill-gotten gain was probably on a par with political machines throughout the rest of the country. It doesn't excuse the depredations of the Tweed Ring, for example, to point out they were of a piece with the era—with the Whiskey Ring, the Union Pacific Ring, the Erie Ring—expanding circles of corruption that occasionally overlapped. America was up for grabs. George Templeton Strong damned the entire New York State legislature as the "Sanhedrin of rascality," a title it more than lived up to during the struggle over the Erie Railroad, when men on both sides of the aisle openly sold their votes.

What was different in New York City was the size

of the trough. In the second half of the nineteenth century, New York mushroomed from a fair-sized seaport to sprawling metropolis, the money market of North America. Romancing the dollar was the city's passion and pastime. "All the world over," wrote one observer in 1872, "poverty is a misfortune. In New York it is a crime."

Plunkitt, whose life encompassed this transformation, was acutely aware of its implications. "It makes me tired," he complains, "to hear of old codgers back in the thirties or forties boastin' that they retired from politics without a dollar except what they earned in their profession or business. If they lived today, with all the existin' opportunities, they would be just the same as twentieth-century politicians."

By the turn of the century, when Plunkitt's words were taken down, the equation of Tammany with the Irish was ironclad. Plunkitt himself, overcoming any temptation to tribal self-effacement (a lapse that few if any of New York's ethnic groups have ever been accused of), declares that the "Irish was born to rule." This destiny, however, was decidedly unclear a half century before, and it is worth remembering that the vaunted Machine ran on tracks set in place by old-stock Americans. The Irish were the rank-and-file majority for at least a generation before one of their own, Honest John Kelly, became the Boss.

Tammany began as a red-blooded patriotic fraternity that took its name from a long-vanished Indian chief. Dedicated to keeping alive the ideals of the Revolution and resisting any resurgence of Tory snobbery and aristocracy, its members paraded in Indian garb and addressed each other with titles like "Brave," or "Sachem," or "Wiskinkie." At this stage, it could have evolved into a house tabby, as tame as the Shriners, instead of into the feared political tiger it became. Not until Aaron Burr took hold of the leash did Tammany's true stripes begin to show.

Although the symbol of the ferocious Bengal tiger wasn't attached to Tammany until Boss Tweed (it had been the logo of the volunteer fire company he headed), it was Burr who gave Tammany its fighting spirit, fashioning a political instrument with which to rule New York and challenge Federalist control of the national government. Burr organized Tammany—or, as officially incorporated, "The Society of St. Tammany or Columbian Order in the City of New York"—around the inner circle of sachems who became the controlling body of the city's anti-Federalist party (known then as Republicans, later as Democrats), and he made sure it was prepared to do whatever was necessary to win.

In 1812, the Society built its first headquarters, or wigwam, at the corner of Nassau and Frankfort, and this hall and its successors became a symbol of the whole Tammany organization. The advent of Jacksonian democracy, along with the abolition in 1822 of property qualifications for New York voters (at least male white ones), required the Hall to reach out to the city's workingmen and, tentatively at first, to the growing number of immigrants.

By the time of Plunkitt's birth in 1842, the rising tide of immigration had made the Irish a constituency that couldn't be ignored. Native-born Americans of every political stripe had an almost instinctually negative reaction to the rapidly expanding number of papist foreigners. But some, like Fernando Wood, a prototypical urban boss, wily, pragmatic, unscrupulous, were able to swallow their distaste in the interests of political practicality. Wood quickly grasped that with their votes, the Irish held the key that turned the lock of electoral victory.

Over the years, a good deal has been written about Tammany Hall and the Irish. Much of it has proceeded on the notion that though (contrary to Plunkitt's boast) the Irish weren't born to rule, they were uniquely equipped to make full use of the American political system. According to this theory, thanks to the mass political movement begun in Ireland by Daniel O'Connell in the 1820s and continuing into the 1840s—a movement aimed at gaining civil rights for Ireland's Catholic majority and, subsequently, at repeal of the union with Great Britain—the Irish landed in America endowed with the organizational skills they needed to turn their numbers to immediate and full advantage.

There is no doubt that O'Connell mobilized the masses as no European political leader had ever done before. But the exact relationship between that experience and the Irish involvement in Tammany is easier invoked than described. Take the case of Plunkitt. Residing in a shantytown in the vicinity of what is now Central Park, Plunkitt's family preceded to America by a few years the vast influx of Irish driven to America by the Great Famine of the 1840s. As a result of this catastrophe, the Irish were decimated by hunger and disease, and over two million, a quarter of the country's population, fled.

The bulk of these emigrants were from the townlands of the south and west. They were a people with no experience of urban or village life, uneducated and unskilled, steeped in the traditions and rhythms of a primitive agricultural economy. Deeply resentful, often violently so, of the Protestant Ascendancy that had monopolized power and wealth in Ireland, a bitterness etched deep by the acid ordeal of the Famine, they poured into the port of New York, crowding into fetid cellars and hovels, swelling the dirt-floored shantytowns in which the Plunkitts had already taken up residence.

We have no records of what the Plunkitts and their neighbors thought about their prospects in America. There were no diarists or memorialists among them. But we know that as well as being a people of few material resources, their arrival in America brought about a powerful reaction. Of this they were quickly made aware. In 1844, soon after Plunkitt saw the first light of day, New York City elected John Harper as Mayor. Harper, a co-founder of the publishing house that still bears his name, was elected on an anti-Catholic, anti-immigrant ticket. His victory was part of a nationwide surge of suspicion and resentment that coalesced into the largest and, for a while, most successful third-party movement in American history.

In New York City, as elsewhere, the battle lines were drawn: on one side the mass of newcomers who had little to recommend them beyond the sheer force of their numbers; on the other the descendants of the country's original white settlers, who were horrified and threatened by the invasion of hordes of ragtag foreigners who filled the almshouses and prisons.

It would seem that whatever effect Daniel O'Connell might have had, the Irish were drawn to American politics by purely practical and situational considerations. Like the Jewish immigrants who would create the American film industry, the Irish followed the path of least resistance. They went where they had the best chance of entry. Politics also allowed them to translate a real, if unquantifiable, cultural emphasis on sociability—on song and on talk—into a usable asset.

Plunkitt's own rise in the world is instructive in this regard. Bereft of education or connections, yet unwilling to resign himself to a lifetime as a Paddy laborer in the city's shambles, he set his sights on politics. He began, he tells us, "by workin' around the district headquarters and hustlin' about the polls on election day." Soon enough, after seeing for himself how the system ran, he went to a cousin and announced, " 'Tommy, I'm goin' to be a politician, and I want to get a followin'; can I count on you?' He said: 'Sure, George.' That's how I started in business. I got a marketable commodity—one vote."

The personal pragmatism encapsulated in Plunkitt's self-described entry into politics may well telescope and simplify a longer and more nuanced process. (Then again, maybe it doesn't.) Yet it is so utterly devoid of any patina of patriotism or idealism that it is hard to believe he made it up. In fact, in its unadorned directness it seems to summarize the oft-repeated assertion that, other than taking care of themselves, the Irish didn't know what to do with political power once they took it.

Plunkitt and many of the Irish of his time would have been bewildered by such a charge. They believed they knew perfectly well what to do with power: first, get it; and once you get it, keep it. They never claimed they had some master plan for socioeconomic reform, and they undoubtedly intuited that the American system looked far more benignly on corruption than radicalism, especially when practiced or preached by immigrant outsiders.

Living in a new country, in the aftermath of the Famine, the Irish employed political power as a buckler of community solidarity and survival, a means with which to shield themselves from the attacks of their enemies, and as a sword with which to strike back. They used the Democratic Party the way they used the Catholic Church, as a rallying point and redoubt, a place in which they gained the resources and discipline to recover from the shattering dislocation endured in their mass exodus from the ancient, familiar patterns of rural life to the freewheeling, winner-take-all environment of urban America.

There wasn't much room for great causes and grand ideas. Romantic Ireland never had much of a chance in the Hall. Tammany was about practical things: about jobs, bread, influence; about the neighborhood kid who needed a lawyer; about the fees paid a subcontractor; and about the hundred cases of champagne and two hundred kegs of beer waiting in the basement of the Hall for those who endured four hours of July Fourth speechifying. Neither Kelly nor Croker nor Murphy were ever in danger of being bathed in the heroic light of, say, a Charles Stewart Parnell. But unlike their cousins back in Ireland, the Irish of Tammany never became the impotent, disappointed romantics found in James Joyce's masterful story of post-Parnell Ireland, "Ivy Day in the Committee Room."

The men who ran Tammany commanded the loyalty of their followers because of their power to overcome the enemy at the polls and to disburse the fruits—or spoils—of their electoral victories. The greatest testament to their success was the ability of the Organization to survive their demise. The Boss might die or flee or go to jail, but the Organization continued. As Croker put it, "A change is a good thing sometimes; but Tammany Hall will be here when we are all gone."

The Bosses were very different men, and Tammany's fortunes varied under each. But they all promised to reward their followers with work. As far as they were able, they kept that promise. In the days before Civil Service, it is estimated that control of the city government meant 12,000 public jobs as well as the ancillary ability to squeeze additional jobs out of the private sector.

Nothing drew Plunkitt's hatred like the Civil Service. The man finds it hard to speak of it and maintain his sanity. But beneath the bluster and the blarney is a very modern concern. Plunkitt claims government jobs as a reward of political victory to be distributed among supporters in need of work. For them it will provide a paycheck and, as important, a toehold on the ladder to respectability. Civil Service defeats this process by restricting access to the already-blessed middle classes who are schooled in a knowledge of the mandarin arcana that, in Plunkitt's view, is the subject of Civil Service exams. ("State all you don't know, and why you don't know it" is Plunkitt's way of summing them up.)

It is not hard to imagine the perverse satisfaction Plunkitt would take in the appearance of affirmative action and the attempt of socially committed, good-hearted liberals to undo the strict Civil Service standards their intellectual ancestors worked so hard to put in place. While he would never approve a program insulated from the direct effect of politics, it is inconceivable that he wouldn't bless any effort to subvert the Civil Service and give the jobs to the people most in need of them.

At the root of much of Tammany's success was the identification with the city's immigrant poor and working classes. Plunkitt and others grew rich on it. As crass and self-serving as this often was, it was also real and powerful. The people weren't fools, at least, as Lincoln framed it, not all of the time. They heard and saw enough to know what Tammany was up to. On occasion their patience was exhausted and they voted to throw the rascals out. But they perceived in Tammany an institution that, if sometimes insincere, was never condescending in the way many middle-class and upper-class reformers were.

There is a scene in Stephen Crane's novella "Maggie, A Girl of the Streets," that sums up this awareness. A tough street kid wanders into a storefront mission "where a man composed his sermons of 'you's.' Once a philosopher asked this man why he did not say 'we' instead of 'you.' The man replied, 'What?' " Tammany never made this mistake.

Tammany was always *we, us,* always doing the people the service of treating them as if they were somebodies. Consider Plunkitt's small but revealing observation on the Wall Street janitors who determined the electoral outcome in the Battery district. Where a middle-class reformer might have seen a pack of ignorant, mopwielding immigrants, Plunkitt sees a proud collection of men who know the significance of their vote. "Even I," he confesses, "might have trouble holding them."

Or consider Johnny Ahearn, leader in the Fourth District on the lower East Side. His constituents, Plunkitt tells us, were "about half Irishmen and half Jews," a division that bothered Ahearn not at all. According to Plunkitt, Ahearn was "as popular with one race as the other. He eats corned beef and kosher meat with equal nonchalance, and it's all the same to him whether he takes off his hat in the church or pulls it down over his ears in the synagogue." When Ahearn died, people in his district sat *shiva* and the street peddlers overturned their carts in a sign of mourning. Of how many reformers could this be said?

The people paid a price for their support of Tammany. Maybe in the end, in some ways, they might have been materially better off heeding the gospel of the reformers. But for all its excesses, for all its thievery and knavery, Tammany afforded the poor what the rich and well-off had denied them throughout history: respect.

Richard Croker said as much in his famous interview with W. T. Stead in 1897. Tammany, he said, was the only organization that met the poor man on his own turf and treated him as an equal: "Think of the hundreds of foreigners dumped into our city. They are too old to go to school. There is not a mugwump who would shake hands with them . . . Tammany looks after them for the sake of their vote, grafts them upon the Republic, makes citizens of them in short; and although you may not like our motives or our methods, what other agency is there by which so long a row could have been hoed so quickly or so well? If we go down into the gutter, it is because there are men in the gutter, and you have got to go where they are if you are to do anything with them."

Croker told a half-truth. Tammany worked the

streets and gutters, but it didn't have to descend from any heights to do so. This is where Tammany came from, and though he retired to the life of an English country gentleman, this is where Croker began his existence in New York, in a shantytown not far from Plunkitt's. Neither Croker nor Plunkitt had any distance to travel to understand where the poor came from; it required no act of the imagination, no leap of sympathetic feeling. And because of this they knew that as long as they didn't strut about with the refined hauteur of the upper classes, the poor were not only likely to forgive them their trespasses, but to cheer them on, the lead runners in a race the denizens of the slums hoped their own children would one day get to run.

The irony is that Tammany's end came not because it resisted the forces of economic progressivism and reform, but because it joined them. Under Charlie Murphy, Tammany swung its support behind a legislative agency that pushed government regulation and protection into areas it had never gone before. Murphy's protegés, Robert Wagner and Al Smith, became prototypes of a new kind of urban politician, streetwise as well as honest, pushing programs designed to improve the condition of people's lives in material ways. Eventually, with the election of Franklin Roosevelt as president in 1932, New York's agenda became the nation's.

It is the received wisdom that Charlie Murphy's death in 1924 (fittingly enough, the same year as Plunkitt's) marked the beginning of the end for Tammany. The Organization fell into the hands of epigones who brought the Seabury investigation down upon their heads, eventually descending into associations with petty gamblers and big-time racketeers. Tammany was made irrelevant by the evolution of a new American political order and became a kind of vestigial organ, like the appendix, capable of doing harm, but unable to make any positive contribution to the body politic. Finally, and mercifully, it was removed. Or so it is said.

There is, however, another version of Tammany's denouement that seems more in keeping with the true trajectory of its development. In 1922, with Murphy's blessing, the Bronx Democratic organization chose as its leader Edward Flynn, an educated, well-mannered, suave Irish American. Murphy obviously liked Flynn and saw in him, perhaps, the next stage of Tammany's existence. Leading an organization one step removed physically, psychically and, in many cases, economically from the immigrant neighborhoods of Manhattan, Flynn had none of the flamboyance of a Jimmy Walker. Just as smart as Walker, Flynn was quieter, steadier, and divorced from the pervasive corruption Walker and company thrived on.

Flynn's highly efficient, disciplined Bronx Machine won elections with even greater regularity than the New York Yankees, that other great Bronx machine, won ball games. Flynn's team played according to the old Tammany rules of district leaders and neighborhood captains, but Flynn had his sights set on a bigger game. He formed a close relationship with Franklin Roosevelt, helping him win the governorship of New York and then doing all he could to elect him president. Flynn stayed a trusted confidant of FDR's. In 1944, it was Flynn who put Truman on the ticket as vice-president.

Nobody ever accused Ed Flynn of not knowing what to do with power once he got it. He worked to put the New Deal in place and kept his full support behind the social legislation that brought an unprecedented degree of security and opportunity to ordinary Americans. With the passage of those reforms, he also helped open a path for his constituents to leave the

Bronx and its urban precincts altogether, passing into the greener pastures of the suburbs, the Promised Land the immigrants had come seeking.

Tammany didn't wither into extinction after Murphy died. Flynn took up the mantle; wore it successfully, regally. He was the true last emperor. The Machine survived long enough after his death to be an early and important supporter of John F. Kennedy, but the glory days were over. Everybody knew it.

What some seem to forget is that the Machine conspired in its own demise. It supported the very legislation that removed its vital role as a quasi-agency of social welfare and legal aid. It bowed before the monstrous regiment of urban planners and their coldblooded schemes for demolishing the old neighborhoods and girding the city with highways whose sole intent was to ease the commute from the suburbs.

Plunkitt was lucky to pass away when he did. He went out attended by a full complement of friends, and even a few enemies. Sacred Heart Church, the *Times* reported, was crowded with politicians: "Among them were John R. Voorhis, Grand Sachem of the Society of Tammany; 'Big Tom' Foley, William Holly and John F. Curry, members of the Council of Sachems; Murray Hulbert, President of the Board of Aldermen; Charles H. Hussey, Tammany leader of the Third Assembly District; The McManus, who succeeded Plunkitt as leader of the Fifth Assembly District; Alderman Charles J. McManus; former United States Senator James A. O'Gorman . . ." All in all, a real-life last hurrah. A cortege of twenty-one automobiles followed the hearse from Plunkitt's home to the church.

Fate smiled on George Washington Plunkitt. It allowed him to travel from a shantytown crowded with Famine refugees to a life of comfort and, almost, respectability. He lived in a time when the city kept growing and booming, and the pie always seemed to get bigger and richer. The Depression, television, the superhighway were hidden from him. Yet Plunkitt sensed trouble ahead. In words that ring with lament as well as prophecy, he saw a day when his world would disappear: "Ignorant people are always talkin' against party bosses, but just wait till the bosses are gone! Then, and not until then, will they get the right sort of epitaphs, as Patrick Henry or Robert Emmet said."

Part of that epitaph was already written at the time of Plunkitt's death. It is contained in this wise, intemperate, hilarious, outrageous little book.

—Peter Quinn

PREFACE

THIS volume discloses the mental operations of perhaps the most thoroughly practical politician of the day—George Washington Plunkitt, Tammany leader of the Fifteenth Assembly District, Sachem of the Tammany Society and Chairman of the Elections Committee of Tammany Hall, who has held the offices of State Senator, Assemblyman, Police Magistrate, County Supervisor and Alderman, and who boasts of his record in filling four public offices in one year and drawing salaries from three of them at the same time.

The discourses that follow were delivered by him from his rostrum, the bootblack stand in the County Court House, at various times in the last half-dozen years. Their absolute frankness and vigorous unconventionality of thought and expression charmed me. Plunkitt said right out what all practical politicians think but are afraid to say. Some of the discourses I published as interviews in the *New York Evening Post,* the *New York Sun,* the *New York World,* and the *Boston Transcript.* They were reproduced in newspapers throughout the country and several of them, notably the talks on "The Curse of Civil Service Reform" and "Honest Graft and Dishonest Graft," became subjects of discussion in the United States Senate and in college lectures. There seemed to be a general recognition of Plunkitt as a striking type of the practical politician, a politician, moreover, who dared to say publicly what others in his class whisper among themselves in the City Hall corridors and the hotel lobbies.

I thought it a pity to let Plunkitt's revelations of himself—as frank in their way as Rousseau's *Confessions*—perish in the files of the newspapers; so I collected the talks I had published, added several new ones, and now give to the world in this volume a system of political philosophy which is as unique as it is refreshing.

No New Yorker needs to be informed who George Washington Plunkitt is. For the information of others, the following sketch of his career is given. He was born, as he proudly tells, in Central Park—that is, in the territory now included in the park. He began life as a driver of a cart, then became a butcher's boy, and later went into the butcher business for himself. How he entered politics he explains in one of his discourses. His advancement was rapid. He was in the Assembly soon after he cast his first vote and has held office most of the time for forty years.

In 1870, through a strange combination of circumstances, he held the places of Assemblyman, Alderman, Police Magistrate and County Supervisor and drew three salaries at once—a record unexampled in New York politics.

Plunkitt is now a millionaire. He owes his fortune mainly to his political pull, as he confesses in "Honest Graft and Dishonest Graft." He is in the contracting, transportation, real estate, and every other business out of which he can make money. He has no office. His headquarters is the County Court House bootblack stand. There he receives his constituents, transacts his general business and pours forth his philosophy.

Plunkitt has been one of the great powers in Tammany Hall for a quarter of a century. While he was in the Assembly and the State Senate he was one of the most influential members and introduced the bills that provided for the outlying parks of New York City, the Harlem River Speedway, the Washington Bridge, the 155th Street Viaduct, the grading of Eighth Avenue north of Fifty-seventh Street, additions to the Museum of Natural History, the West Side Court, and many other important public improvements. He is one of the closest friends and most valued advisers of Charles F. Murphy, leader of Tammany Hall.

—William L. Riordon

A TRIBUTE TO PLUNKITT BY
THE LEADER OF TAMMANY HALL

SENATOR PLUNKITT is a straight organization man. He believes in party government; he does not indulge in cant and hypocrisy and he is never afraid to say exactly what he thinks. He is a believer in thorough political organization and all-the-year-around work, and he holds to the doctrine that, in making appointments to office, party workers should be preferred if they are fitted to perform the duties of the office. Plunkitt is one of the veteran leaders of the organization; he has always been faithful and reliable, and he has performed valuable services for Tammany Hall.

—Charles F. Murphy

PLUNKITT

of

TAMMANY HALL

Honest Graft and Dishonest Graft

EVERYBODY is talkin' these days about Tammany men growin' rich on graft, but nobody thinks of drawin' the distinction between honest graft and dishonest graft. There's all the difference in the world between the two. Yes, many of our men have grown rich in politics. I have myself. I've made a big fortune out of the game, and I'm gettin' richer every day, but I've not gone in for dishonest graft—blackmailin' gamblers, saloonkeepers, disorderly people, etc.—and neither has any of the men who have made big fortunes in politics.

There's an honest graft, and I'm an example of how it works. I might sum up the whole thing by sayin': "I seen my opportunities and I took 'em."

Just let me explain by examples. My party's in power in the city, and it's goin' to undertake a lot of public improvements. Well, I'm tipped off, say, that they're going to lay out a new park at a certain place.

I see my opportunity and I take it. I go to that place and I buy up all the land I can in the neighborhood. Then the board of this or that makes its plan public, and there is a rush to get my land, which nobody cared particular for before.

Ain't it perfectly honest to charge a good price and make a profit on my investment and foresight? Of course, it is. Well, that's honest graft.

Or supposin' it's a new bridge they're goin' to build. I get tipped off and I buy as much property as I can

3

that has to be taken for approaches. I sell at my own price later on and drop some more money in the bank.

Wouldn't you? It's just like lookin' ahead in Wall Street or in the coffee or cotton market. It's honest graft, and I'm lookin' for it every day in the year. I will tell you frankly that I've got a good lot of it, too.

I'll tell you of one case. They were goin' to fix up a big park, no matter where. I got on to it, and went lookin' about for land in that neighborhood.

I could get nothin' at a bargain but a big piece of swamp, but I took it fast enough and held on to it. What turned out was just what I counted on. They couldn't make the park complete without Plunkitt's swamp, and they had to pay a good price for it. Anything dishonest in that?

Up in the watershed I made some money, too. I bought up several bits of land there some years ago and made a pretty good guess that they would be bought up for water purposes later by the city.

Somehow, I always guessed about right, and shouldn't I enjoy the profit of my foresight? It was rather amusin' when the condemnation commissioners came along and found piece after piece of the land in the name of George Plunkitt of the Fifteenth Assembly District, New York City. They wondered how I knew just what to buy. The answer is—I seen my opportunity and I took it. I haven't confined myself to land; anything that pays is in my line.

For instance, the city is repavin' a street and has several hundred thousand old granite blocks to sell. I am on hand to buy, and I know just what they are worth.

How? Never mind that. I had a sort of monopoly of this business for a while, but once a newspaper tried to do me. It got some outside men to come over from Brooklyn and New Jersey to bid against me.

Was I done? Not much. I went to each of the men and said: "How many of these 250,000 stones do you want?" One said 20,000, and another wanted 15,000, and the other wanted 10,000. I said: "All right, let me bid for the lot, and I'll give each of you all you want for nothin'."

They agreed, of course. Then the auctioneer yelled: "How much am I bid for these 250,000 fine pavin' stones?"

"Two dollars and fifty cents," says I.

"Two dollars and fifty cents!" screamed the auctioneer. "Oh, that's a joke! Give me a real bid."

He found the bid was real enough. My rivals stood silent. I got the lot for $2.50 and gave them their share. That's how the attempt to do Plunkitt ended, and that's how all such attempts end.

I've told you how I got rich by honest graft. Now, let me tell you that most politicians who are accused of robbin' the city get rich the same way.

They didn't steal a dollar from the city treasury. They just seen their opportunities and took them. That is why, when a reform administration comes in and spends a half million dollars in tryin' to find the public robberies they talked about in the campaign, they don't find them.

The books are always all right. The money in the city treasury is all right. Everything is all right. All they can show is that the Tammany heads of departments looked after their friends, within the law, and gave them what opportunities they could to make honest graft. Now, let me tell you that's never goin' to hurt Tammany with the people. Every good man looks after his friends, and any man who doesn't isn't likely to be popular. If I have a good thing to hand out in private life, I give it to a friend. Why shouldn't I do the same in public life?

Another kind of honest graft. Tammany has raised a good many salaries. There was an awful howl by the reformers, but don't you know that Tammany gains ten votes for every one it lost by salary raisin'?

The Wall Street banker thinks it shameful to raise a department clerk's salary from $1500 to $1800 a year, but every man who draws a salary himself says: "That's all right. I wish it was me." And he feels very much like votin' the Tammany ticket on election day, just out of sympathy.

Tammany was beat in 1901 because the people were deceived into believin' that it worked dishonest graft. They didn't draw a distinction between dishonest and honest graft, but they saw that some Tammany men grew rich, and supposed they had been robbin' the city treasury or levyin' blackmail on disorderly houses, or workin' in with the gamblers and lawbreakers.

As a matter of policy, if nothing else, why should the Tammany leaders go into such dirty business, when there is so much honest graft lyin' around when they are in power? Did you ever consider that?

Now, in conclusion, I want to say that I don't own a dishonest dollar. If my worst enemy was given the job of writin' my epitaph when I'm gone, he couldn't do more than write:

"George W. Plunkitt. He Seen His Opportunities, and He Took 'Em."

How to Become a Statesman

THERE'S thousands of young men in this city who will go to the polls for the first time next November. Among them will be many who have watched the careers of successful men in politics, and who are longin' to make names and fortunes for themselves at the same game. It is to these youths that I want to give advice. First, let me say that I am in a position to give what the courts call expert testimony on the subject. I don't think you can easily find a better example than I am of success in politics. After forty years' experience at the game I am—well, I'm George Washington Plunkitt. Everybody knows what figure I cut in the greatest organization on earth, and if you hear people say that I've laid away a million or so since I was a butcher's boy in Washington Market, don't come to me for an indignant denial. I'm pretty comfortable, thank you.

Now, havin' qualified as an expert, as the lawyers say, I am goin' to give advice free to the young men who are goin' to cast their first votes, and who are lookin' forward to political glory and lots of cash. Some young men think they can learn how to be successful in politics from books, and they cram their heads with all sorts of college rot. They couldn't make a bigger mistake. Now, understand me, I ain't sayin' nothin' against colleges. I guess they'll have to exist as long as there's bookworms, and I suppose they do

7

some good in a certain way, but they don't count in politics. In fact, a young man who has gone through the college course is handicapped at the outset. He may succeed in politics, but the chances are 100 to 1 against him.

Another mistake: some young men think that the best way to prepare for the political game is to practice speakin' and becomin' orators. That's all wrong. We've got some orators in Tammany Hall, but they're chiefly ornamental. You never heard of Charlie Murphy delivering a speech, did you? Or Richard Croker, or John Kelly, or any other man who has been a real power in the organization? Look at the thirty-six district leaders of Tammany Hall today. How many of them travel on their tongues? Maybe one or two, and they don't count when business is doin' at Tammany Hall. The men who rule have practiced keepin' their tongues still, not exercisin' them. So you want to drop the orator idea unless you mean to go into politics just to perform the skyrocket act.

Now, I've told you what not to do; I guess I can explain best what to do to succeed in politics by tellin' you what I did. After goin' through the apprenticeship of the business while I was a boy by workin' around the district headquarters and hustlin' about the polls on election day, I set out when I cast my first vote to win fame and money in New York City politics. Did I offer my services to the district leader as a stump-speaker? Not much. The woods are always full of speakers. Did I get up a book on municipal government and show it to the leader? I wasn't such a fool. What I did was to get some marketable goods before goin' to the leaders. What do I mean by marketable goods? Let me tell you: I had a cousin, a young man who didn't take any particular interest in politics. I went to him and said: "Tommy, I'm goin' to be a politician, and I want to get a followin'; can I count on you?" He said: "Sure, George." That's how I started in business. I got a marketable commodity—one vote. Then I went to the district leader and told him I could command two votes on election day, Tommy's and my own. He smiled on me and told me to go ahead. If I had offered him a speech or a bookful of learnin', he would have said, "Oh, forget it!"

That was beginnin' business in a small way, wasn't it? But that is the only way to become a real lastin' statesman. I soon branched out. Two young men in the flat next to mine were school friends. I went to them, just as I went to Tommy, and they agreed to stand by me. Then I had a followin' of three voters and I began to get a bit chesty. Whenever I dropped into district headquarters, everybody shook hands with me, and the leader one day honored me by lightin' a match for my cigar. And so it went on like a snowball rollin' down a hill. I worked the flat-house that I lived in from the basement to the top floor, and I got about a dozen young men to follow me. Then I tackled the next house and so on down the block and around the corner. Before long I had sixty men back of me, and formed the George Washington Plunkitt Association.

What did the district leader say then when I called at headquarters? I didn't have to call at headquarters. He came after me and said: "George, what do you want? If you don't see what you want, ask for it. Wouldn't you like to have a job or two in the departments for your friends?" I said: "I'll think it over; I haven't yet decided what the George Washington Plunkitt Association will do in the next campaign." You ought to have seen how I was courted and petted then by the leaders of the rival organizations. I had marketable goods and there was bids for them from all sides, and I was a risin' man in politics. As time went on, and my association grew, I thought I would like to go to the Assembly. I just had to hint at what I wanted, and three different organizations offered me the nomination. Afterwards, I went to the Board of

Aldermen, then to the State Senate, then became leader of the district, and so on up and up till I became a statesman.

That is the way and the only way to make a lastin' success in politics. If you are goin' to cast your first vote next November and want to go into politics, do as I did. Get a followin', if it's only one man, and then go to the district leader and say: "I want to join the organization. I've got one man who'll follow me through thick and thin." The leader won't laugh at your one-man followin'. He'll shake your hand warmly, offer to propose you for membership in his club, take you down to the corner for a drink and ask you to call again. But go to him and say: "I took first prize at college in Aristotle; I can recite all Shakespeare forwards and backwards; there ain't nothin' in science that ain't as familiar to me as blockades on the elevated roads and I'm the real thing in the way of silver-tongued orators." What will he answer? He'll probably say: "I guess you are not to blame for your misfortunes, but we have no use for you here."

The Curse of Civil Service Reform

THIS civil service law is the biggest fraud of the age. It is the curse of the nation. There can't be no real patriotism while it lasts. How are you goin' to interest our young men in their country if you have no offices to give them when they work for their party? Just look at things in this city today. There are ten thousand good offices, but we can't get at more than a few hundred of them. How are we goin' to provide for the thousands of men who worked for the Tammany ticket? It can't be done. These men were full of patriotism a short time ago. They expected to be servin' their city, but when we tell them that we can't place them, do you think their patriotism is goin' to last? Not much. They say: "What's the use of workin' for your country anyhow? There's nothin' in the game." And what can they do? I don't know, but I'll tell you what I do know. I know more than one young man in past years who worked for the ticket and was just overflowin' with patriotism, but when he was knocked out by the civil service humbug he got to hate his country and became an Anarchist.

This ain't no exaggeration. I have good reason for sayin' that most of the Anarchists in this city today are men who ran up against civil service examinations. Isn't it enough to make a man sour on his country when he wants to serve it and won't be allowed unless he answers a lot of fool questions about the number of cubic inches of water in the Atlantic and the quality of sand in the Sahara desert? There was once a bright young man in my district who tackled one of these examinations. The next I heard of him he had settled down in Herr Most's saloon smokin' and drinkin' beer and talkin' socialism all day. Before that time he had never drank anything but whisky. I knew what was comin' when a young Irishman drops whisky and takes to beer and long pipes in a German saloon. That young man is today one of the wildest Anarchists in town. And just to think! He might be a patriot but for that cussed civil service.

Say, did you hear about that Civil Service Reform Association kickin' because the tax commissioners want to put their fifty-five deputies on the exempt list, and fire the outfit left to them by Low? That's civil service for you. Just think! Fifty-five Republicans and mugwumps holdin' $3000 and $4000 and $5000 jobs in the tax department when 1555 good Tammany men are ready and willin' to take their places! It's an outrage! What did the people mean when they voted for Tammany? What is representative government, anyhow? Is it all a fake that this is a government of the people, by the people and for the people? If it isn't a fake, then why isn't the people's voice obeyed and Tammany men put in all the offices?

When the people elected Tammany, they knew just what they were doin'. We didn't put up any false pretenses. We didn't go in for humbug civil service and all that rot. We stood as we have always stood, for rewardin' the men that won the victory. They call that the spoils system. All right; Tammany is for the spoils system, and when we go in we fire every anti-Tammany man from office that can be fired under the law. It's an elastic sort of law and you can bet it will be stretched to the limit. Of course the Republican State Civil Service Board will stand in the way of our local Civil Service Commission all it can; but say!—suppose we carry the State sometime, won't we fire the upstate Board all right? Or we'll make it work in harmony with the local board, and that means that Tammany will get everything in sight. I know that the civil service humbug is stuck into the constitution, too, but, as Tim Campbell said: "What's the constitution among friends?"

Say, the people's voice is smothered by the cursed civil service law; it is the root of all evil in our government. You hear of this thing or that thing goin' wrong in the nation, the State or the city. Look down beneath the surface and you can trace everything wrong to civil service. I have studied the subject and I know. The civil service humbug is underminin' our institutions and if a halt ain't called soon this great republic will tumble down like a Park Avenue house when they were buildin' the subway, and on its ruins will rise another Russian government.

This is an awful serious proposition. Free silver and the tariff and imperialism and the Panama Canal are triflin' issues when compared to it. We could worry along without any of these things, but civil service is sappin' the foundation of the whole shootin' match. Let me argue it out for you. I ain't up on sillygisms, but I can give you some arguments that nobody can answer.

First, this great and glorious country was built up by political parties; second, parties can't hold together if their workers don't get the offices when they win; third, if the parties go to pieces, the government they built up must go to pieces, too; fourth, then there'll be h—— to pay.

Could anything be clearer than that? Say, honest now; can you answer that argument? Of course you won't deny that the government was built up by the great parties. That's history, and you can't go back of the returns. As to my second proposition, you can't deny that either. When parties can't get offices, they'll bust. They ain't far from the bustin' point now, with all this civil service business keepin' most of the good things from them. How are you goin' to keep up patriotism if this thing goes on? You can't do it. Let me tell you that patriotism has been dying out fast for the last twenty years. Before then when a party won, its workers got everything in sight. That was somethin' to make a man patriotic. Now, when a party wins and its men come forward and ask for their rewards, the reply is, "Nothin' doin', unless you can answer a list of questions about Egyptian mummies and how many years it will take for a bird to wear out a mass of iron as big as the earth by steppin' on it once in a century?"

I have studied politics and men for forty-five years, and I see how things are driftin'. Sad indeed is the change that has come over the young men, even in my district, where I try to keep up the fire of patriotism by gettin' a lot of jobs for my constituents, whether Tammany is in or out. The boys and men don't get excited any more when they see a United States flag or hear "The Star-Spangled Banner." They don't care no more for firecrackers on the Fourth of July. And why should they? What is there in it for them? They know that no matter how hard they work for their country in a campaign, the jobs will go to fellows who can tell about the mummies and the bird steppin' on the iron. Are you surprised then that the young men of the country are beginnin' to look coldly on the flag and don't care to put up a nickel for firecrackers?

Say, let me tell of one case. After the battle of San Juan Hill, the Americans found a dead man with a light complexion, red hair and blue eyes. They could see he wasn't a Spaniard, although he had on a Spanish uniform. Several officers looked him over, and then a private of the Seventy-first Regiment saw him and yelled, "Good Lord, that's Flaherty." That man grew up in my district, and he was once the most patriotic American boy on the West Side. He couldn't see a flag without yellin' himself hoarse.

Now, how did he come to be lying dead with a Spanish uniform on? I found out all about it, and I'll vouch for the story. Well, in the municipal campaign of 1897, that young man, chockful of patriotism, worked day and night for the Tammany ticket. Tammany won, and the young man determined to devote his life to the service of the city. He picked out a place that would suit him, and sent in his application to the head of department. He got a reply that he must take a civil service examination to get the place. He didn't know what these examinations were, so he went, all lighthearted, to the Civil Service Board. He read the questions about the mummies, the bird on the iron, and all the other fool questions—and he left that office an enemy of the country that he had loved so well. The mummies and the bird blasted his patriotism. He went to Cuba, enlisted in the Spanish army at the breakin' out of the war, and died fightin' his country.

That is but one victim of the infamous civil service. If that young man had not run up against the civil examination, but had been allowed to serve his country as he wished, he would be in a good office today, drawin' a good salary. Ah, how many young men have had their patriotism blasted in the same way!

Now, what is goin' to happen when civil service crushes out patriotism? Only one thing can happen: the republic will go to pieces. Then a czar or a sultan will turn up, which brings me to the fourthly of my argument—that is, there will be h—— to pay. And that ain't no lie.

Reformers Only
Mornin' Glories

COLLEGE professors and philosophers who go up in a
balloon to think are always discussin' the question:
"Why Reform Administrations Never Succeed Themselves!" The reason is plain to anybody who has
learned the a, b, c of politics.

I can't tell just how many of these movements I've
seen started in New York during my forty years in
politics, but I can tell you how many have lasted more
than a few years—none. There have been reform committees of fifty, of sixty, of seventy, of one hundred
and all sorts of numbers that started out to do up
the regular political organizations. They were mornin'
glories—looked lovely in the mornin' and withered up
in a short time, while the regular machines went on
flourishin' forever, like fine old oaks. Say, that's the
first poetry I ever worked off. Ain't it great?

Just look back a few years. You remember the People's Municipal League that nominated Frank Scott
for mayor in 1890? Do you remember the reformers
that got up that league? Have you ever heard of them
since? I haven't. Scott himself survived because he had
always been a first-rate politician, but you'd have to
look in the newspaper almanacs of 1891 to find out
who made up the People's Municipal League. Oh, yes!
I remember one name: Ollie Teall; dear, pretty Ollie
and his big dog. They're about all that's left of the
League.

Now take the reform movement of 1894. A lot of good politicians joined in that—the Republicans, the State Democrats, the Stecklerites and the O'Brienites, and they gave us a lickin', but the real reform part of the affair, the Committee of Seventy that started the thing goin', what's become of those reformers? What's become of Charles Stewart Smith? Where's Bangs? Do you ever hear of Cornell, the iron man, in politics now? Could a search party find R. W. G. Welling? Have you seen the name of Fulton McMahon or McMahon Fulton—I ain't sure which—in the papers lately? Or Preble Tucker? Or—but it's no use to go through the list of the reformers who said they sounded in the death knell of Tammany in 1894. They're gone for good, and Tammany's pretty well, thank you. They did the talkin' and posin', and the politicians in the movement got all the plums. It's always the case.

The Citizens' Union has lasted a little bit longer than the reform crowd that went before them, but that's because they learned a thing or two from us. They learned how to put up a pretty good bluff—and bluff counts a lot in politics. With only a few thousand members, they had the nerve to run the whole Fusion movement, make the Republicans and other organizations come to their headquarters to select a ticket and dictate what every candidate must do or not do. I love nerve, and I've had a sort of respect for the Citizens' Union lately, but the Union can't last. Its people haven't been trained to politics, and whenever Tammany calls their bluff they lay right down. You'll never hear of the Union again after a year or two.

And, by the way, what's become of the good government clubs, the political nurseries of a few years ago? Do you ever hear of Good Government Club D and P and Q and Z any more? What's become of the infants who were to grow up and show us how to govern the city? I know what's become of the nursery

that was started in my district. You can find pretty
much the whole outfit over in my headquarters, Washington Hall.

The fact is that a reformer can't last in politics. He
can make a show for a while, but he always comes
down like a rocket. Politics is as much a regular business as the grocery or the dry-goods or the drug business. You've got to be trained up to it or you're sure
to fail. Suppose a man who knew nothing about the
grocery trade suddenly went into the business and
tried to conduct it according to his own ideas.
Wouldn't he make a mess of it? He might make a
splurge for a while, as long as his money lasted, but
his store would soon be empty. It's just the same with
a reformer. He hasn't been brought up in the difficult
business of politics and he makes a mess of it every
time.

I've been studyin' the political game for forty-five
years, and I don't know it all yet. I'm learnin' somethin' all the time. How, then, can you expect what
they call "business men" to turn into politics all at
once and make a success of it? It is just as if I went
up to Columbia University and started to teach Greek.
They usually last about as long in politics as I would
last at Columbia.

You can't begin too early in politics if you want to
succeed at the game. I began several years before I
could vote, and so did every successful leader in Tammany Hall. When I was twelve years old I made myself useful around the district headquarters and did
work at all the polls on election day. Later on, I hus-
tled about gettin' out voters who had jags on or who
were too lazy to come to the polls. There's a hundred
ways that boys can help, and they get an experience
that's the first real step in statesmanship. Show me a
boy that hustles for the organization on election day,
and I'll show you a comin' statesman.

That's the a, b, c of politics. It ain't easy work to

get up to y and z. You have to give nearly all your time and attention to it. Of course, you may have some business or occupation on the side, but the great business of your life must be politics if you want to succeed in it. A few years ago Tammany tried to mix politics and business in equal quantities, by havin' two leaders for each district, a politician and a business man. They wouldn't mix. They were like oil and water. The politician looked after the politics of his district; the business man looked after his grocery store or his milk route, and whenever he appeared at an executive meeting, it was only to make trouble. The whole scheme turned out to be a farce and was abandoned mighty quick.

Do you understand now, why it is that a reformer goes down and out in the first or second round, while a politician answers to the gong every time? It is because the one has gone into the fight without trainin', while the other trains all the time and knows every fine point of the game.

New York City Is Pie for the Hayseeds

THIS city is ruled entirely by the hayseed legislators at Albany. I've never known an upstate Republican who didn't want to run things here, and I've met many thousands of them in my long service in the Legislature. The hayseeds think we are like the Indians to the National Government—that is, sort of wards of the State, who don't know how to look after ourselves and have to be taken care of by the Republicans of St. Lawrence, Ontario, and other backwoods counties. Why should anybody be surprised because ex-Governor Odell comes down here to direct the Republican machine? Newburg ain't big enough for him. He, like all the other upstate Republicans, wants to get hold of New York City. New York is their pie.

Say, you hear a lot about the downtrodden people of Ireland and the Russian peasants and the sufferin' Boers. Now, let me tell you that they have more real freedom and home rule than the people of this grand and imperial city. In England, for example, they make a pretense of givin' the Irish some self-government. In this State the Republican government makes no pretense at all. It says right out in the open: "New York City is a nice big fat Goose. Come along with your carvin' knives and have a slice." They don't pretend to ask the Goose's consent.

We don't own our streets or our docks or our water-front or anything else. The Republican Legislature and

Governor run the whole shootin' match. We've got to eat and drink what they tell us to eat and drink, and have got to choose our time for eatin' and drinkin' to suit them. If they don't feel like takin' a glass of beer on Sunday, we must abstain. If they have not got any amusements up in their backwoods, we mustn't have none. We've got to regulate our whole lives to suit them. And then we have to pay their taxes to boot.

Did you ever go up to Albany from this city with a delegation that wanted anything from the Legislature? No? Well, don't. The hayseeds who run all the committees will look at you as if you were a child that didn't know what it wanted, and will tell you in so many words to go home and be good and the Legislature will give you whatever it thinks is good for you. They put on a sort of patronizing air, as much as to say, "These children are an awful lot of trouble. They're wantin' candy all the time, and they know that it will make them sick. They ought to thank goodness that they have us to take care of them." And if you try to argue with them, they'll smile in a pityin' sort of way as if they were humorin' a spoiled child.

But just let a Republican farmer from Chemung or Wayne or Tioga turn up at the Capital. The Republican Legislature will make a rush for him and ask him what he wants and tell him if he doesn't see what he wants to ask for it. If he says his taxes are too high, they reply to him: "All right, old man, don't let that worry you. How much do you want us to take off?"

"I guess about fifty per cent will about do for the present," says the man. "Can you fix me up?"

"Sure," the Legislature agrees. "Give us somethin' harder, don't be bashful. We'll take off sixty per cent if you wish. That's what we're here for."

Then the Legislature goes and passes a law increasin' the liquor tax or some other tax in New York City, takes a half of the proceeds for the State Treasury and cuts down the farmers' taxes to suit. It's as easy as rollin' off a log—when you've got a good workin' majority and no conscience to speak of.

Let me give you another example. It makes me hot under the collar to tell about this. Last year some hayseeds along the Hudson River, mostly in Odell's neighborhood, got dissatisfied with the docks where they landed their vegetables, brickbats, and other things they produce in the river counties. They got together and said: "Let's take a trip down to New York and pick out the finest dock we can find. Odell and the Legislature will do the rest." They did come down here, and what do you think they hit on? The finest dock in my district. Invaded George W. Plunkitt's district without sayin' as much as "by your leave." Then they called on Odell to put through a bill givin' them this dock, and he did.

When the bill came before Mayor Low I made the greatest speech of my life. I pointed out how the Legislature could give the whole waterfront to the hayseeds over the head of the Dock Commissioner in the same way, and warned the Mayor that nations had rebelled against their governments for less. But it was no go. Odell and Low were pards and—well, my dock was stolen.

You heard a lot in the State campaign about Odell's great work in reducin' the State tax to almost nothin', and you'll hear a lot more about it in the campaign next year. How did he do it? By cuttin' down the expenses of the State Government? Oh, no! The expenses went up. He simply performed the old Republican act of milkin' New York City. The only difference was that he nearly milked the city dry. He not only ran up the liquor tax, but put all sorts of taxes on corporations, banks, insurance companies, and everything in sight that could be made to give up. Of course, nearly the whole tax fell on the city. Then Odell went through the country districts and said:

"See what I have done for you. You ain't got any more taxes to pay the State. Ain't I a fine feller?"

Once a farmer in Orange County asked him: "How did you do it, Ben?"

"Dead easy," he answered. "Whenever I want any money for the State Treasury, I know where to get it," and he pointed toward New York City.

And then all the Republican tinkerin' with New York City's charter. Nobody can keep up with it. When a Republican mayor is in, they give him all sorts of power. If a Tammany mayor is elected next fall I wouldn't be surprised if they changed the whole business and arranged it so that every city department should have four heads, two of them Republicans. If we make a kick, they would say: "You don't know what's good for you. Leave it to us. It's our business."

To Hold Your District:
Study Human Nature
and Act Accordin'

THERE'S only one way to hold a district: you must study human nature and act accordin'. You can't study human nature in books. Books is a hindrance more than anything else. If you have been to college, so much the worse for you. You'll have to unlearn all you learned before you can get right down to human nature, and unlearnin' takes a lot of time. Some men can never forget what they learned at college. Such men may get to be district leaders by a fluke, but they never last.

To learn real human nature you have to go among the people, see them and be seen. I know every man, woman, and child in the Fifteenth District, except them that's been born this summer—and I know some of them, too. I know what they like and what they don't like, what they are strong at and what they are weak in, and I reach them by approachin' at the right side.

For instance, here's how I gather in the young men. I hear of a young feller that's proud of his voice, thinks that he can sing fine. I ask him to come around to Washington Hall and join our Glee Club. He comes and sings, and he's a follower of Plunkitt for life. Another young feller gains a reputation as a baseball player in a vacant lot. I bring him into our baseball club. That fixes him. You'll find him workin' for my ticket at the polls next election day. Then there's the feller that likes rowin' on the river, the young feller that makes a name as a waltzer on his block, the young feller that's handy with his dukes—I rope them all in by givin' them opportunities to show themselves off. I don't trouble them with political arguments. I just study human nature and act accordin'.

But you may say this game won't work with the high-toned fellers, the fellers that go through college and then join the Citizens' Union. Of course it wouldn't work. I have a special treatment for them. I ain't like the patent medicine man that gives the same medicine for all diseases. The Citizens' Union kind of a young man! I love him! He's the daintiest morsel of the lot, and he don't often escape me.

Before telling you how I catch him, let me mention that before the election last year, the Citizens' Union said they had four hundred or five hundred enrolled voters in my district. They had a lovely headquarters, too, beautiful roll-top desks and the cutest rugs in the world. If I was accused of havin' contributed to fix up the nest for them, I wouldn't deny it under oath. What do I mean by that? Never mind. You can guess from the sequel, if you're sharp.

Well, election day came. The Citizens' Union's candidate for Senator, who ran against me, just polled five votes in the district, while I polled something more than 14,000 votes. What became of the 400 or 500 Citizens' Union enrolled voters in my district? Some people guessed that many of them were good Plunkitt men all along and worked with the Cits just to bring them into the Plunkitt camp by election day. You can guess that way, too, if you want to. I never contradict stories about me, especially in hot weather. I just call your attention to the fact that on last election day 395 Citizens' Union enrolled voters in my district were missin' and unaccounted for.

I tell you frankly, though, how I have captured some of the Citizens' Union's young men. I have a plan that never fails. I watch the City Record to see when there's civil service examinations for good things. Then I take my young Cit in hand, tell him all about the good thing and get him worked up till he goes and takes an examination. I don't bother about him any more. It's a cinch that he comes back to me in a few days and asks to join Tammany Hall. Come over to Washington Hall some night and I'll show you a list of names on our rolls marked "C.S." which means, "bucked up against civil service."

As to the older voters, I reach them, too. No, I don't send them campaign literature. That's rot. People can get all the political stuff they want to read—and a good deal more, too—in the papers. Who reads speeches, nowadays, anyhow? It's bad enough to listen to them. You ain't goin' to gain any votes by stuffin' the letter boxes with campaign documents. Like as not you'll lose votes for there's nothin' a man hates more than to hear the letter carrier ring his bell and go to the letter box expectin' to find a letter he was lookin' for, and find only a lot of printed politics. I met a man this very mornin' who told me he voted the Democratic State ticket last year just because the Republicans kept crammin' his letter box with campaign documents.

What tells in holdin' your grip on your district is to go right down among the poor families and help them in the different ways they need help. I've got a regular system for this. If there's a fire in Ninth, Tenth, or Eleventh Avenue, for example, any hour of the day or night, I'm usually there with some of my election district captains as soon as the fire engines. If a family is burned out I don't ask whether they are Republicans or Democrats, and I don't refer them to the Charity Organization Society, which would investigate their case in a month or two and decide they were worthy of help about the time they are dead from starvation. I just get quarters for them, buy clothes for them if their clothes were burned up, and fix them up till they get things runnin' again. It's philanthropy, but it's politics, too—mighty good politics. Who can tell how many votes one of these fires bring me? The poor are the most grateful people in the world, and, let me tell you, they have more friends in their neighborhoods than the rich have in theirs.

If there's a family in my district in want I know it before the charitable societies do, and me and my men are first on the ground. I have a special corps to look up such cases. The consequence is that the poor look up to George W. Plunkitt as a father, come to him in trouble—and don't forget him on election day.

Another thing, I can always get a job for a deservin' man. I make it a point to keep on the track of jobs, and it seldom happens that I don't have a few up my sleeve ready for use. I know every big employer in the district and in the whole city, for that matter, and they ain't in the habit of sayin' no to me when I ask them for a job.

And the children—the little roses of the district! Do I forget them? Oh, no! They know me, every one of them, and they know that a sight of Uncle George and candy means the same thing. Some of them are the best kind of vote-getters. I'll tell you a case. Last year a little Eleventh Avenue rosebud, whose father is a Republican, caught hold of his whiskers on election day and said she wouldn't let go till he'd promise to vote for me. And she didn't.

On *The Shame of the Cities*

I'VE been readin' a book by Lincoln Steffens on *The Shame of the Cities*. Steffens means well but, like all reformers, he don't know how to make distinctions. He can't see no difference between honest graft and dishonest graft and, consequent, he gets things all mixed up. There's the biggest kind of a difference between political looters and politicians who make a fortune out of politics by keepin' their eyes wide open. The looter goes in for himself alone without considerin' his organization or his city. The politician looks after his own interests, the organization's interests, and the city's interests all at the same time. See the distinction? For instance, I ain't no looter. The looter hogs it. I never hogged. I made my pile in politics, but, at the same time, I served the organization and got more big improvements for New York City than any other livin' man. And I never monkeyed with the penal code.

The difference between a looter and a practical politician is the difference between the Philadelphia Republican gang and Tammany Hall. Steffens seems to think they're both about the same; but he's all wrong. The Philadelphia crowd runs up against the penal code. Tammany don't. The Philadelphians ain't satisfied with robbin' the bank of all its gold and paper money. They stay to pick up the nickels and pennies and the cop comes and nabs them. Tammany ain't no such fool. Why, I remember, about fifteen or twenty years ago, a Republican superintendent of the Philadelphia almshouse stole the zinc roof off the buildin' and sold it for junk. That was carryin' things to excess. There's a limit to everything, and the Philadelphia Republicans go beyond the limit. It seems like they can't be cool and moderate like real politicians. It ain't fair, therefore, to class Tammany men with the Philadelphia gang. Any man who undertakes to write political books should never for a moment lose sight of the distinction between honest graft and dishonest graft, which I explained in full in another talk. If he puts all kinds of graft on the same level, he'll make the fatal mistake that Steffens made and spoil his book.

A big city like New York or Philadelphia or Chicago might be compared to a sort of Garden of Eden, from a political point of view. It's an orchard full of beautiful apple trees. One of them has got a big sign on it, marked: "Penal Code Tree—Poison." The other trees have lots of apples on them for all. Yet the fools go to the Penal Code Tree. Why? For the reason, I guess, that a cranky child refuses to eat good food and chews up a box of matches with relish. I never had any temptation to touch the Penal Code Tree. The other apples are good enough for me, and O Lord! how many of them there are in a big city!

Steffens made one good point in his book. He said he found that Philadelphia, ruled almost entirely by Americans, was more corrupt than New York, where the Irish do almost all the governin'. I could have told him that before he did any investigatin' if he had come to me. The Irish was born to rule, and they're the honestest people in the world. Show me the Irishman who would steal a roof off an almshouse! He don't exist. Of course, if an Irishman had the political pull and the roof was much worn, he might get the city authorities to put on a new one and get the contract for it himself, and buy the old roof at a bargain—but that's honest graft. It's goin' about the thing like a gentleman, and there's more money in it than in tearin' down an old roof and cartin' it to the junkman's—more money and no penal code.

One reason why the Irishman is more honest in politics than many Sons of the Revolution is that he is grateful to the country and the city that gave him protection and prosperity when he was driven by oppression from the Emerald Isle. Say, that sentence is fine, ain't it? I'm goin' to get some literary feller to work it over into poetry for next St. Patrick's Day dinner.

Yes, the Irishman is grateful. His one thought is to serve the city which gave him a home. He has this thought even before he lands in New York, for his friends here often have a good place in one of the city departments picked out for him while he is still in the old country. Is it any wonder that he has a tender spot in his heart for old New York when he is on its salary list the mornin' after he lands?

Now, a few words on the general subject of the so-called shame of cities. I don't believe that the government of our cities is any worse, in proportion to opportunities, than it was fifty years ago. I'll explain what I mean by "in proportion to opportunities." A half a century ago, our cities were small and poor. There wasn't many temptations lyin' around for politicians. There was hardly anything to steal, and hardly any opportunities for even honest graft. A city could count its money every night before goin' to bed, and if three cents was missin', all the fire bells would be rung. What credit was there in bein' honest under them circumstances? It makes me tired to hear of old codgers back in the thirties or forties boastin' that they retired from politics without a dollar except what they earned in their profession or business. If they lived today, with all the existin' opportunities, they would be just the same as twentieth-century politicians. There ain't any more honest people in the world just now than the convicts in Sing Sing. Not one of them steals anything. Why? Because they can't. See the application?

Understand, I ain't defendin' politicians of today who steal. The politician who steals is worse than a thief. He is a fool. With the grand opportunities all around for the man with a political pull, there's no excuse for stealin' a cent. The point I want to make is that if there is some stealin' in politics, it don't mean that the politicians of 1905 are, as a class, worse than them of 1835. It just means that the old-timers had nothin' to steal, while the politicians now are surrounded by all kinds of temptations and some of them naturally—the fool ones—buck up against the penal code.

Ingratitude in Politics

THERE'S no crime so mean as ingratitude in politics, but every great statesman from the beginnin' of the world has been up against it. Caesar had his Brutus; that king of Shakespeare's—Leary, I think you call him—had his own daughters go back on him; Platt had his Odell, and I've got my "The" McManus. It's a real proof that a man is great when he meets with political ingratitude. Great men have a tender, trustin' nature. So have I, outside of the contractin' and real estate business. In politics I have trusted men who have told me they were my friends, and if traitors have turned up in my camp—well, I only had the same experience as Caesar, Leary, and the others. About my Brutus. McManus, you know, has seven brothers and they call him "The" because he is the boss of the lot, and to distinguish him from all other McManuses. For several years he was a political bushwhacker. In campaigns he was sometimes on the fence, sometimes on both sides of the fence, and sometimes under the fence. Nobody knew where to find him at any particular time, and nobody trusted him—that is, nobody but me. I thought there was some good in him after all and that, if I took him in hand, I could make a man of him yet.

I did take him in hand, a few years ago. My friends told me it would be the Brutus-Leary business all over

again, but I didn't believe them. I put my trust in
"The." I nominated him for the Assembly, and he was
elected. A year afterwards, when I was runnin' for re-
election as Senator, I nominated him for the Assembly
again on the ticket with me. What do you think hap-
pened? We both carried the Fifteenth Assembly District, but he ran away ahead of me. Just think! Ahead
of me in my own district! I was just dazed. When I
began to recover, my election district captains came
to me and said that McManus had sold me out with
the idea of knockin' me out of the Senatorship, and
then tryin' to capture the leadership of the district. I
couldn't believe it. My trustin' nature couldn't imagine
such treachery.

I sent for McManus and said, with my voice trem-
blin' with emotions: "They say you have done me dirt,
'The.' It can't be true. Tell me it ain't true."

"The" almost wept as he said he was innocent.

"Never have I done you dirt, George," he declared.
"Wicked traitors have tried to do you. I don't know
just who they are yet, but I'm on their trail, and I'll
find them or abjure the name of 'The' McManus. I'm
goin' out right now to find them."

Well, "The" kept his word as far as goin' out and
findin' the traitors was concerned. He found them all
right—and put himself at their head. Oh, no! He
didn't have to go far to look for them. He's got them
gathered in his clubrooms now, and he's doin' his best
to take the leadership from the man that made him.
So you see that Caesar and Leary and me's in the
same boat, only I'll come out on top while Caesar and
Leary went under.

Now let me tell you that the ingrate in politics never
flourishes long. I can give you lots of examples. Look
at the men who done up Roscoe Conkling when he
resigned from the United States Senate and went to
Albany to ask for re-election! What's become of
them? Passed from view like a movin' picture. Who

took Conkling's place in the Senate? Twenty dollars even that you can't remember his name without looking in the almanac. And poor old Platt! He's down and out now and Odell is in the saddle, but that don't mean that he'll always be in the saddle. His enemies are workin' hard all the time to do him, and I wouldn't be a bit surprised if he went out before the next State campaign.

The politicians who make a lastin' success in politics are the men who are always loyal to their friends, even up to the gate of State prison, if necessary; men who keep their promises and never lie. Richard Croker used to say that tellin' the truth and stickin' to his friends was the political leader's stock in trade. Nobody ever said anything truer, and nobody lived up to it better than Croker. That is why he remained leader of Tammany Hall as long as he wanted to. Every man in the organization trusted him. Sometimes he made mistakes that hurt in campaigns, but they were always on the side of servin' his friends.

It's the same with Charles F. Murphy. He has always stood by his friends even when it looked like he would be downed for doin' so. Remember how he stuck to McClellan in 1903 when all the Brooklyn leaders were against him, and it seemed as if Tammany was in for a grand smash-up! It's men like Croker and Murphy that stay leaders as long as they live; not men like Brutus and McManus.

Now I want to tell you why political traitors, in New York City especially, are punished quick. It's because the Irish are in a majority. The Irish, above all people in the world, hates a traitor. You can't hold them back when a traitor of any kind is in sight and, rememberin' old Ireland, they take particular delight in doin' up a political traitor. Most of the voters in my district are Irish or of Irish descent; they've spotted "The" McManus, and when they get a chance at him at the polls next time, they won't do a thing to him.

The question has been asked: Is a politician ever justified in goin' back on his district leader? I answer: "No; as long as the leader hustles around and gets all the jobs possible for his constituents." When the voters elect a man leader, they make a sort of a contract with him. They say, although it ain't written out: "We've put you here to look out for our interests. You want to see that this district gets all the jobs that's comin' to it. Be faithful to us, and we'll be faithful to you."

The district leader promises and that makes a solemn contract. If he lives up to it, spends most of his time chasin' after places in the departments, picks up jobs from railroads and contractors for his followers, and shows himself in all ways a true statesman, then his followers are bound in honor to uphold him, just as they're bound to uphold the Constitution of the United States. But if he only looks after his own interests or shows no talent for scenting out jobs or ain't got the nerve to demand and get his share of the good things that are goin', his followers may be absolved from their allegiance and they may up and swat him without bein' put down as political ingrates.

Reciprocity in Patronage

WHENEVER Tammany is whipped at the polls, the people set to predictin' that the organization is goin' to smash. They say we can't get along without the offices and that the district leaders are goin' to desert wholesale. That was what was said after the throwdowns in 1894 and 1901. But it didn't happen, did it? Not one big Tammany man deserted, and today the organization is stronger than ever.

How was that? It was because Tammany has more than one string to its bow.

I acknowledge that you can't keep an organization together without patronage. Men ain't in politics for nothin'. They want to get somethin' out of it.

But there is more than one kind of patronage. We lost the public kind, or a greater part of it, in 1901, but Tammany has an immense private patronage that keeps things goin' when it gets a setback at the polls.

Take me, for instance. When Low came in, some of my men lost public jobs, but I fixed them all right. I don't know how many jobs I got for them on the surface and elevated railroads—several hundred.

I placed a lot more on public works done by contractors, and no Tammany man goes hungry in my district. Plunkitt's O.K. on an application for a job is never turned down, for they all know that Plunkitt and Tammany don't stay out long. See!

Let me tell you, too, that I got jobs from Republicans in office—Federal and otherwise. When Tammany's on top I do good turns for the Republicans. When they're on top they don't forget me.

Me and the Republicans are enemies just one day in the year—election day. Then we fight tooth and nail. The rest of the time it's live and let live with us.

On election day I try to pile up as big a majority as I can against George Wanmaker, the Republican leader of the Fifteenth. Any other day George and I are the best of friends. I can go to him and say: "George, I want you to place this friend of mine." He says: "All right, Senator." Or vice versa.

You see, we differ on tariffs and currencies and all them things, but we agree on the main proposition that when a man works in politics, he should get something out of it.

The politicians have got to stand together this way or there wouldn't be any political parties in a short time. Civil service would gobble up everything, politicians would be on the bum, the republic would fall and soon there would be the cry of "Vevey le roi!"

The very thought of this civil service monster makes my blood boil. I have said a lot about it already, but another instance of its awful work just occurs to me.

Let me tell you a sad but true story. Last Wednesday a line of carriages wound into Calvary Cemetery. I was in one of them. It was the funeral of a young man from my district—a bright boy that I had great hopes of.

When he went to school, he was the most patriotic boy in the district. Nobody could sing "The Star-Spangled Banner" like him, nobody was as fond of waving a flag, and nobody shot off as many firecrackers on the Fourth of July. And when he grew up he made up his mind to serve his country in one of the city departments. There was no way of gettin' there without passin' a civil service examination. Well, he went down to the civil service office and tackled the fool questions. I saw him next day—it was Memorial Day, and soldiers were marchin' and flags flyin' and people cheerin'.

Where was my young man? Standin' on the corner, scowlin' at the whole show. When I asked him why he was so quiet, he laughed in a wild sort of way and said: "What rot all this is!"

Just then a band came along playing "Liberty." He laughed wild again and said: "Liberty? Rats!"

I don't guess I need to make a long story of it.

From the time that young man left the civil service office he lost all patriotism. He didn't care no more for his country. He went to the dogs.

He ain't the only one. There's a gravestone over some bright young man's head for every one of them infernal civil service examinations. They are underminin' the manhood of the nation and makin' the Declaration of Independence a farce. We need a new Declaration of Independence—independence of the whole fool civil service business.

I mention all this now to show why it is that the politicians of two big parties help each other along, and why Tammany men are tolerably happy when not in power in the city. When we win I won't let any deservin' Republican in my neighborhood suffer from hunger or thirst, although, of course, I look out for my own people first.

Now, I've never gone in for nonpartisan business, but I do think that all the leaders of the two parties should get together and make an open, nonpartisan fight against civil service, their common enemy. They could keep up their quarrels about imperialism and free silver and high tariff. They don't count for much alongside of civil service, which strikes right at the root of the government. The time is fast coming when civil service or the politicians will have to go. And it will be here sooner than they expect if the politicians don't unite, drop all them minor issues for a while and make a stand against the civil service flood that's sweepin' over the country like them floods out West.

Brooklynites Natural-
Born Hayseeds

SOME people are wonderin' why it is that the Brooklyn Democrats have been sidin' with David B. Hill and the upstate crowd. There's no cause for wonder. I have made a careful study of the Brooklynite, and I can tell you why. It's because a Brooklynite is a natural-born hayseed, and can never become a real New Yorker. He can't be trained into it. Consolidation didn't make him a New Yorker, and nothin' on earth can. A man born in Germany can settle down and become a good New Yorker. So can an Irishman; in fact, the first word an Irish boy learns in the old country is "New York," and when he grows up and comes here, he is at home right away. Even a Jap or a Chinaman can become a New Yorker, but a Brooklynite never can.

And why? Because Brooklyn don't seem to be like any other place on earth. Once let a man grow up amidst Brooklyn's cobblestones, with the odor of Newton Creek and Gowanus Canal ever in his nostrils, and there's no place in the world for him except Brooklyn. And even if he don't grow up there; if he is born there and lives there only in his boyhood and then moves away, he is still beyond redemption. In one of my speeches in the Legislature, I gave an example of this, and it's worth repeatin' now. Soon after I became a leader on the West Side, a quarter of a century ago, I came across a bright boy, about seven years old, who had just been brought over from Brooklyn by his parents. I took an interest in the boy, and when he grew up I brought him into politics. Finally, I sent him to the Assembly from my district. Now remember that the boy was only seven years old when he left Brooklyn, and was twenty-three when he went to the Assembly. You'd think he had forgotten all about Brooklyn, wouldn't you? I did, but I was dead wrong. When that young fellow got into the Assembly he paid no attention to bills or debates about New York City. He didn't even show any interest in his own district. But just let Brooklyn be mentioned, or a bill be introduced about Gowanus Canal, or the Long Island Railroad, and he was all attention. Nothin' else on earth interested him.

The end came when I caught him—what do you think I caught him at? One mornin' I went over from the Senate to the Assembly chamber, and there I found my young man readin'—actually readin' a Brooklyn newspaper! When he saw me comin' he tried to hide the paper, but it was too late. I caught him dead to rights, and I said to him: "Jimmy, I'm afraid New York ain't fascinatin' enough for you. You had better move back to Brooklyn after your present term." And he did. I met him the other day crossin' the Brooklyn Bridge, carryin' a hobbyhorse under one arm, and a doll's carriage under the other, and lookin' perfectly happy.

McCarren and his men are the same way. They can't get it into their heads that they are New Yorkers, and just tend naturally toward supportin' Hill and his hayseeds against Murphy. I had some hopes of McCarren till lately. He spends so much of his time over here and has seen so much of the world that I thought he might be an exception, and grow out of his Brooklyn surroundings, but his course at Albany shows that there is no exception to the rule. Say, I'd rather take a Hottentot in hand to bring up as a good New Yorker

than undertake the job with a Brooklynite. Honest,
I would.

And, by the way, come to think of it, is there really
any upstate Democrats left? It has never been proved
to my satisfaction that there is any. I know that some
upstate members of the State committee call themselves Democrats. Besides these, I know at least six
more men above the Bronx who make a livin' out of
professin' to be Democrats, and I have just heard of
some few more. But if there is any real Democrats up
the State, what becomes of them on election day?
They certainly don't go near the polls or they vote the
Republican ticket. Look at the last three State elections! Roosevelt piled up more than 100,000 majority
above the Bronx; Odell piled up about 160,000 majority the first time he ran and 131,000 the second time.
About all the Democratic votes cast were polled in
New York City. The Republicans can get all the votes
they want up the State. Even when we piled up
123,000 majority for Coler in the city in 1902, the Republicans went it 8000 better above the Bronx.

That's why it makes me mad to hear about upstate
Democrats controllin' our State convention, and sayin'
who we shall choose for President. It's just like Staten
Island undertakin' to dictate to a New York City convention. I remember once a Syracuse man came to
Richard Croker at the Democratic Club, handed him
a letter of introduction and said: "I'm lookin' for a
job in the Street Cleanin' Department; I'm backed by
a hundred upstate Democrats." Croker looked hard at
the man a minute and then said: "Upstate Democrats!
Upstate Democrats! I didn't know there was any upstate Democrats. Just walk up and down a while till I
see what an upstate Democrat looks like."

Another thing. When a campaign is on, did you ever
hear of an upstate Democrat makin' a contribution?
Not much. Tammany has had to foot the whole bill,
and when any of Hill's men came down to New York

to help him in the campaign, we had to pay their board. Whenever money is to be raised, there's nothin' doin' up the State. The Democrats there—always providin' that there is any Democrats there—take to the woods. Supposin' Tammany turned over the campaigns to the Hill men and then held off, what would happen? Why, they would have to hire a shed out in the suburbs of Albany for a headquarters, unless the Democratic National Committee put up for the campaign expenses. Tammany's got the votes and the cash. The Hill crowd's only got hot air.

Tammany Leaders
Not Bookworms

You hear a lot of talk about the Tammany district leaders bein' illiterate men. If illiterate means havin' common sense, we plead guilty. But if they mean that the Tammany leaders ain't got no education and ain't gents they don't know what they're talkin' about. Of course, we ain't all bookworms and college professors. If we were, Tammany might win an election once in four thousand years. Most of the leaders are plain American citizens, of the people and near to the people, and they have all the education they need to whip the dudes who part their name in the middle and to run the City Government. We've got bookworms, too, in the organization. But we don't make them district leaders. We keep them for ornaments on parade days.

Tammany Hall is a great big machine, with every part adjusted delicate to do its own particular work. It runs so smooth that you wouldn't think it was a complicated affair, but it is. Every district leader is fitted to the district he runs and he wouldn't exactly fit any other district. That's the reason Tammany never makes the mistake the Fusion outfit always makes of sendin' men into the districts who don't know the people, and have no sympathy with their peculiarities. We don't put a silk stockin' on the Bowery, nor do we make a man who is handy with his fists leader of the Twenty-ninth. The Fusionists make about the same sort of a mistake that a repeater made at an election in Albany several years ago. He was hired to go to the polls early in a half-dozen election districts and vote on other men's names before these men reached the polls. At one place, when he was asked his name by the poll clerk, he had the nerve to answer "William Croswell Doane."

"Come off. You ain't Bishop Doane," said the poll clerk.

"The hell I ain't, you——!" yelled the repeater.

Now, that is the sort of bad judgment the Fusionists are guilty of. They don't pick men to suit the work they have to do.

Take me, for instance. My district, the Fifteenth, is made up of all sorts of people, and a cosmopolitan is needed to run it successful. I'm a cosmopolitan. When I get into the silk-stockin' part of the district, I can talk grammar and all that with the best of them. I went to school three winters when I was a boy, and I learned a lot of fancy stuff that I keep for occasions. There ain't a silk stockin' in the district who ain't proud to be seen talkin' with George Washington Plunkitt, and maybe they learn a thing or two from their talks with me. There's one man in the district, a big banker, who said to me one day: "George, you can sling the most vigorous English I ever heard. You remind me of Senator Hoar of Massachusetts." Of course, that was puttin' it on too thick; but say, honest, I like Senator Hoar's speeches. He once quoted in the United States Senate some of my remarks on the curse of civil service, and, though he didn't agree with me altogether, I noticed that our ideas are alike in some things, and we both have the knack of puttin' things strong, only he put on more frills to suit his audience.

As for the common people of the district, I am at home with them at all times. When I go among them, I don't try to show off my grammar, or talk about the Constitution, or how many volts there is in electricity or make it appear in any way that I am better educated than they are. They wouldn't stand for that sort of thing. No; I drop all monkeyshines. So you see, I've got to be several sorts of a man in a single day, a lightnin' change artist, so to speak. But I am one sort of man always in one respect: I stick to my friends high and low, do them a good turn whenever I get a chance, and hunt up all the jobs going for my constituents. There ain't a man in New York who's got such a scent for political jobs as I have. When I get up in the mornin' I can almost tell every time whether a job has become vacant over night, and what department it's in and I'm the first man on the ground to get it. Only last week I turned up at the office of Water Register Savage at 9 A.M. and told him I wanted a vacant place in his office for one of my constituents. "How did you know that O'Brien had got out?" he asked me. "I smelled it in the air when I got up this mornin'," I answered. Now, that was the fact. I didn't know there was a man in the department named O'Brien, much less that he had got out, but my scent led me to the Water Register's office, and it don't often lead me wrong.

A cosmopolitan ain't needed in all the other districts, but our men are just the kind to rule. There's Dan Finn, in the Battery district, bluff, jolly Dan, who is now on the bench. Maybe you'd think that a court justice is not the man to hold a district like that, but you're mistaken. Most of the voters of the district are the janitors of the big office buildings on lower Broadway and their helpers. These janitors are the most dignified and haughtiest of men. Even I would have trouble in holding them. Nothin' less than a judge on the bench is good enough for them. Dan does the dignity act with the janitors, and when he is with the boys he hangs up the ermine in the closet and becomes a jolly good fellow.

Big Tom Foley, leader of the Second District, fits in exactly, too. Tom sells whisky, and good whisky,

and he is able to take care of himself against a half
dozen thugs if he runs up against them on Cherry Hill
or in Chatham Square. Pat Ryder and Johnnie Ahearn
of the Third and Fourth Districts are just the men
for the places. Ahearn's constituents are about half
Irishmen and half Jews. He is as popular with one
race as with the other. He eats corned beef and kosher
meat with equal nonchalance, and it's all the same to
him whether he takes off his hat in the church or pulls
it down over his ears in the synagogue.

The other downtown leaders, Barney Martin of the
Fifth, Tim Sullivan of the Sixth, Pat Keahon of the
Seventh, Florrie Sullivan of the Eighth, Frank Goodwin of the Ninth, Julius Harburger of the Tenth, Pete
Dooling of the Eleventh, Joe Scully of the Twelfth,
Johnnie Oakley of the Fourteenth, and Pat Keenan of
the Sixteenth are just built to suit the people they
have to deal with. They don't go in for literary business much downtown, but these men are all real gents,
and that's what the people want—even the poorest
tenement dwellers. As you go farther uptown you find
a rather different kind of district leader. There's Vic-
tor Dowling who was until lately the leader of the
Twenty-fourth. He's a lulu. He knows the Latin grammar backward. What's strange, he's a sensible young
fellow, too. About once in a century we come across
a fellow like that in Tammany politics. James J. Martin, leader of the Twenty-seventh, is also something of
a hightoner, and publishes a law paper, while Thomas
E. Rush, of the Twenty-ninth, is a lawyer, and Isaac
Hopper, of the Thirty-first, is a big contractor. The
downtown leaders wouldn't do uptown, and vice versa.
So, you see, these fool critics don't know what they're
talkin' about when they criticize Tammany Hall, the
most perfect political machine on earth.

Dangers of the Dress
Suit in Politics

PUTTIN' on style don't pay in politics. The people won't stand for it. If you've got an achin' for style, sit down on it till you have made your pile and landed a Supreme Court Justiceship with a fourteen-year term at $17,500 a year, or some job of that kind. Then you've got about all you can get out of politics, and you can afford to wear a dress suit all day and sleep in it all night if you have a mind to. But, before you have caught onto your life meal ticket, be simple. Live like your neighbors even if you have the means to live better. Make the poorest man in your district feel that he is your equal, or even a bit superior to you.

Above all things, avoid a dress suit. You have no idea of the harm that dress suits have done in politics. They are not so fatal to young politicians as civil service reform and drink, but they have scores of victims. I will mention one sad case. After the big Tammany victory in 1897, Richard Croker went down to Lakewood to make up the slate of offices for Mayor Van Wyck to distribute. All the district leaders and many more Tammany men went down there, too, to pick up anything good that was goin'. There was nothin' but dress suits at dinner at Lakewood, and Croker wouldn't let any Tammany men go to dinner without them. Well, a bright young West Side politician, who held a three-thousand-dollar job in one of the departments, went to Lakewood to ask Croker for something better. He wore a dress suit for the first time in his life. It was his undoin'. He got stuck on himself. He thought he looked too beautiful for anything, and when he came home he was a changed man. As soon as he got to his house every evenin' he put on that dress suit and set around in it until bedtime. That didn't satisfy him long. He wanted others to see how beautiful he was in a dress suit; so he joined dancin' clubs and began goin' to all the balls that was given in town. Soon he began to neglect his family. Then he took to drinkin', and didn't pay any attention to his political work in the district. The end came in less than a year. He was dismissed from the department and went to the dogs. The other day I met him rigged out almost like a hobo, but he still had a dress-suit vest on. When I asked him what he was doin', he said: "Nothin' at present, but I got a promise of a job en-rollin' voters at Citizens' Union headquarters." Yes, a dress suit had brought him that low!

I'll tell you another case right in my own Assembly District. A few years ago I had as one of my lieuten-ants a man named Zeke Thompson. He did fine work for me and I thought he had a bright future. One day he came to me, said he intended to buy an option on a house, and asked me to help him out. I like to see a young man acquirin' property and I had so much confidence in Zeke that I put up for him on the house.

A month or so afterwards I heard strange rumors. People told me that Zeke was beginnin' to put on style. They said he had a billiard table in his house and had hired Jap servants. I couldn't believe it. The idea of a Democrat, a follower of George Washington Plunkitt in the Fifteenth Assembly District havin' a billiard table and Jap servants! One mornin' I called at the house to give Zeke a chance to clear himself. A Jap opened the door for me. I saw the billiard table. Zeke was guilty! When I got over the shock, I said to Zeke: "You are caught with the goods on. No excuses will go. The Democrats of this district ain't used to dukes and princes and we wouldn't feel comfortable in your company. You'd overpower us. You had better move up to the Nineteenth or Twenty-seventh District, and hang a silk stocking on your door." He went up to the Nineteenth, turned Republican, and was lookin' for an Albany job the last I heard of him.

Now, nobody ever saw me puttin' on any style. I'm the same Plunkitt I was when I entered politics forty years ago. That is why the people of the district have confidence in me. If I went into the stylish business, even I, Plunkitt, might be thrown down in the district. That was shown pretty clearly in the senatorial fight last year. A day before the election, my enemies circulated a report that I had ordered a $10,000 automobile and a $125 dress suit. I sent out contradictions as fast as I could, but I wasn't able to stamp out the infamous slander before the votin' was over, and I suffered some at the polls. The people wouldn't have minded much if I had been accused of robbin' the city treasury, for they're used to slanders of that kind in campaigns, but the automobile and the dress suit were too much for them.

Another thing that people won't stand for is showin' off your learnin'. That's just puttin' on style in another way. If you're makin' speeches in a campaign, talk the language the people talk. Don't try to show how the situation is by quotin' Shakespeare. Shakespeare was all right in his way, but he didn't know anything about Fifteenth District politics. If you know Latin and Greek and have a hankerin' to work them off on somebody, hire a stranger to come to your house and listen to you for a couple of hours; then go out and talk the language of the Fifteenth to the people. I know it's an awful temptation, the hankerin' to show off your learnin'. I've felt it myself, but I always resist it. I know the awful consequences.

On Municipal Ownership

I AM for municipal ownership on one condition: that the civil service law be repealed. It's a grand idea—the city ownin' the railroads, the gas works and all that. Just see how many thousands of new places there would be for the workers in Tammany! Why, there would be almost enough to go around, if no civil service law stood in the way. My plan is this: first get rid of that infamous law, and then go ahead and by degrees get municipal ownership.

Some of the reformers are sayin' that municipal ownership won't do because it would give a lot of patronage to the politicians. How those fellows mix things up when they argue! They're givin' the strongest argument in favor of municipal ownership when they say that. Who is better fitted to run the railroads and the gas plants and the ferries than the men who make a business of lookin' after the interests of the city? Who is more anxious to serve the city? Who needs the jobs more?

Look at the Dock Department! The city owns the docks, and how beautiful Tammany manages them! I can't tell you how many places they provide for our workers. I know there is a lot of talk about dock graft, but that talk comes from the outs. When the Republicans had the docks under Low and Strong, you didn't hear them sayin' anything about graft, did you? No;

they just went in and made hay while the sun shone. That's always the case. When the reformers are out they raise the yell that Tammany men should be sent to jail. When they get in, they're so busy keepin' out of jail themselves that they don't have no time to attack Tammany.

All I want is that municipal ownership be postponed till I get my bill repealin' the civil service law before the next legislature. It would be all a mess if every man who wanted a job would have to run up against a civil service examination. For instance, if a man wanted a job as motorman on a surface car, it's ten to one that they would ask him: "Who wrote the Latin grammar, and, if so, why did he write it? How many years were you at college? Is there any part of the Greek language you don't know? State all you don't know, and why you don't know it. Give a list of all the sciences with full particulars about each one and how it came to be discovered. Write out word for word the last ten decisions of the United States Supreme Court and show if they conflict with the last ten decisions of the police courts of New York City."

Before the would-be motorman left the civil service room, the chances are he would be a raving lunatic. Anyhow I wouldn't like to ride on his car. Just here I want to say one last final word about civil service. In the last ten years I have made an investigation which I've kept quiet till this time. Now I have all the figures together, and I'm ready to announce the result. My investigation was to find out how many civil service reformers and how many politicians were in state prisons. I discovered that there was forty per cent more civil service reformers among the jailbirds. If any legislative committee wants the detailed figures, I'll prove what I say. I don't want to give the figures now, because I want to keep them to back me up when I go to Albany to get the civil service law repealed. Don't you think that when I've had my inning, the civil service law will go down, and the people will see that the politicians are all right, and that they ought to have the job of runnin' things when municipal ownership comes?

One thing more about municipal ownership. If the city owned the railroads, etc., salaries would be sure to go up. Higher salaries is the cryin' need of the day. Municipal ownership would increase them all along the line and would stir up such patriotism as New York City never knew before. You can't be patriotic on a salary that just keeps the wolf from the door. Any man who pretends he can will bear watchin'. Keep your hand on your watch and pocketbook when he's about. But, when a man has a good fat salary, he finds himself hummin' "Hail Columbia," all unconscious and he fancies, when he's ridin' in a trolley car, that the wheels are always sayin': "Yankee Doodle Came to Town." I know how it is myself. When I got my first good job from the city I bought up all the firecrackers in my district to salute this glorious country. I couldn't wait for the Fourth of July. I got the boys on the block to fire them off for me, and I felt proud of bein' an American. For a long time after that I use to wake up nights singin' "The Star-Spangled Banner."

Tammany the Only
Lastin' Democracy

I've seen more than one hundred "Democracies" rise and fall in New York City in the last quarter of a century. At least a half-dozen new so-called Democratic organizations are formed every year. All of them go in to down Tammany and take its place, but they seldom last more than a year or two, while Tammany's like the everlastin' rocks, the eternal hills and the blockades on the "L" road—it goes on forever.

I recall offhand the County Democracy, which was the only real opponent Tammany has had in my time, the Irving Hall Democracy, the New York State Democracy, the German-American Democracy, the Protection Democracy, the Independent County Democracy, the Greater New York Democracy, the Jimmy O'Brien Democracy, the Delicatessen Dealers' Democracy, the Silver Democracy, and the Italian Democracy. Not one of them is livin' today, although I hear somethin' about the ghost of the Greater New York Democracy bein' seen on Broadway once or twice a year.

In the old days of the County Democracy, a new Democratic organization meant some trouble for Tammany—for a time anyhow. Nowadays a new Democracy means nothin' at all except that about a dozen bone-hunters have got together for one campaign only to try to induce Tammany to give them a job or two, or in order to get in with the reformers for the same purpose. You might think that it would

cost a lot of money to get up one of these organizations and keep it goin' for even one campaign, but,
Lord bless you! it costs next to nothin'. Jimmy
O'Brien brought the manufacture of "Democracies"
down to an exact science, and reduced the cost of
production so as to bring it within the reach of all.
Any man with $50 can now have a "Democracy" of
his own.

I've looked into the industry, and can give rock-
bottom figures. Here's the items of cost of a new
"Democracy":

A dinner to twelve bone-hunters	$12.00
A speech on Jeffersonian Democracy	00.00
A proclamation of principles (typewriting)	2.00
Rent of a small room one month for headquarters	12.00
Stationery	2.00
Twelve secondhand chairs	6.00
One secondhand table	2.00
Twenty-nine cuspidors	9.00
Sign painting	5.00
Total	$50.00

Is there any reason for wonder, then, that "Democracies" spring up all over when a municipal campaign
is comin' on? If you land even one small job, you get
a big return on your investment. You don't have to
pay for advertisin' in the papers. The New York papers tumble over one another to give columns to any
new organization that comes out against Tammany. In
describin' the formation of a "Democracy" on the $50
basis, accordin' to the items I give, the papers would
say somethin' like this: "The organization of the Delicatessen Democracy last night threatens the existence
of Tammany Hall. It is a grand move for a new and
pure Democracy in this city. Well may the Tammany
leaders be alarmed; panic has already broke loose in

Fourteenth Street. The vast crowd that gathered at
the launching of the new organization, the stirrin'
speeches and the proclamation of principles mean
that, at last, there is an uprisin' that will end Tammany's career of corruption. The Delicatessen Democracy will open in a few days spacious headquarters
where all true Democrats may gather and prepare for
the fight.''

Say, ain't some of the papers awful gullible about
politics? Talk about come-ons from Iowa or Texas—
they ain't in it with the childlike simplicity of these
papers.

It's a wonder to me that more men don't go into this
kind of manufacturin' industry. It has bigger profits
generally than the green-goods business and none of
the risks. And you don't have to invest as much as
the green-goods men. Just see what good things some
of these "Democracies" got in the last few years! The
New York State Democracy in 1897 landed a Supreme
Court Justiceship for the man who manufactured the
concern—a fourteen-year term at $17,500 a year, that is
$245,000. You see, Tammany was rather scared that year
and was bluffed into givin' this job to get the support
of the State Democracy which, by the way, went out
of business quick and prompt the day after it got this
big plum. The next year the German Democracy
landed a place of the same kind. And then see how
the Greater New York Democracy worked the game
on the reformers in 1901! The men who managed this
concern were former Tammanyites who had lost their
grip; yet they made the Citizens' Union innocents believe that they were the real thing in the way of reformers, and that they had 100,000 votes back of them.
They got the Borough President of Manhattan, the
President of the Board of Aldermen, the Register and
a lot of lesser places. It was the greatest bunco game
of modern times.

And then, in 1894, when Strong was elected mayor,

what a harvest it was for all the little "Democracies" that was made to order that year! Every one of them got somethin' good. In one case, all the nine men in an organization got jobs payin' from $2000 to $5000. I happen to know exactly what it cost to manufacture that organization. It was $42.04. They left out the stationery, and had only twenty-three cuspidors. The extra four cents was for two postage stamps.

The only reason I can imagine why more men don't go into this industry is because they don't know about it. And just here it strikes me that it might not be wise to publish what I've said. Perhaps if it gets to be known what a snap this manufacture of "Democracies" is, all the green-goods men, the bunco-steerers, and the young Napoleons of finance will go into it and the public will be humbugged more than it has been. But, after all, what difference would it make? There's always a certain number of suckers and a certain number of men lookin' for a chance to take them in, and the suckers are sure to be took one way or another. It's the everlastin' law of demand and supply.

Concerning Gas in Politics

SINCE the eighty-cent gas bill was defeated in Albany, everybody's talkin' about senators bein' bribed. Now, I wasn't in the Senate last session, and I don't know the ins and outs of everything that was done, but I can tell you that the legislators are often hauled over the coals when they are all on the level. I've been there and I know. For instance, when I voted in the Senate in 1904, for the Remsen Bill that the newspapers called the "Astoria Gas Grab Bill," they didn't do a thing to me. The papers kept up a howl about all the supporters of the bill bein' bought up by the Consolidated Gas Company, and the Citizens' Union did me the honor to call me the commander-in-chief of the "Black Horse Cavalry."

The fact is that I was workin' for my district all this time, and I wasn't bribed by nobody. There's several of these gashouses in the district, and I wanted to get them over to Astoria for three reasons: first, because they're nuisances; second, because there's no votes in them for me any longer; third, because—well, I had a little private reason which I'll explain further on. I needn't explain how they're nuisances. They're worse than open sewers. Still, I might have stood that if they hadn't degenerated so much in the last few years.

Ah, gashouses ain't what they used to be! Not very long ago, each gashouse was good for a couple of hundred votes. All the men employed in them were Irishmen and Germans who lived in the district. Now, it is all different. The men are dagoes who live across in Jersey and take no interest in the district. What's the use of havin' ill-smellin' gashouses if there's no votes in them?

Now, as to my private reason. Well, I'm a business man and go in for any business that's profitable and honest. Real estate is one of my specialties. I know the value of every foot of ground in my district, and I calculated long ago that if them gashouses was removed, surroundin' property would go up 100 per cent. When the Remsen Bill, providin' for the removal of the gashouses to Queens County came up, I said to myself: "George, hasn't your chance come?" I answered: "Sure." Then I sized up the chances of the bill. I found it was certain to pass the Senate and the Assembly, and I got assurances straight from headquarters that Governor Odell would sign it. Next I came down to the city to find out the mayor's position. I got it straight that he would approve the bill, too.

Can't you guess what I did then? Like any sane man who had my information, I went in and got options on a lot of the property around the gashouses. Well, the bill went through the Senate and the Assembly all right and the mayor signed it, but Odell backslided at the last minute and the whole game fell through. If it had succeeded, I guess I would have been accused of graftin'. What I want to know is, what do you call it when I got left and lost a pot of money?

I not only lost money, but I was abused for votin' for the bill. Wasn't that outrageous? They said I was in with the Consolidated Gas Company and all other kinds of rot, when I was really only workin' for my district and tryin' to turn an honest penny on the side. Anyhow I got a little fun out of the business. When the Remsen Bill was up, I was tryin' to put through a bill of my own, the Spuyten Duyvil Bill, which provided for fillin' in some land under water that the New York Central Railroad wanted. Well, the Remsen managers were afraid of bein' beaten and they went around offerin' to make trades with senators and assemblymen who had bills they were anxious to pass. They came to me and offered six votes for my Spuyten Duyvil Bill in exchange for my vote on the Remsen Bill. I took them up in a hurry, and they felt pretty sore afterwards when they heard I was goin' to vote for the Remsen Bill anyhow.

A word about that Spuyten Duyvil Bill—I was criticized a lot for introducin' it. They said I was workin' in the interest of the New York Central, and was goin' to get the contract for fillin' in. The fact is, that the fillin' in was a good thing for the city, and if it helped the New York Central, too, what of it? The railroad is a great public institution, and I was never an enemy of public institutions. As to the contract, it hasn't come along yet. If it does come, it will find me at home at all proper and reasonable hours, if there is a good profit in sight.

The papers and some people are always ready to find wrong motives in what us statesmen do. If we bring about some big improvement that benefits the city and it just happens, as a sort of coincidence, that we make a few dollars out of the improvement, they say we are grafters. But we are used to this kind of ingratitude. It falls to the lot of all statesmen, especially Tammany statesmen. All we can do is to bow our heads in silence and wait till time has cleared our memories.

Just think of mentionin' dishonest graft in connection with the name of George Washington Plunkitt, the man who gave the city its magnificent chain of parks, its Washington Bridge, its Speedway, its Museum of Natural History, its One Hundred and Fifty-fifth Street Viaduct and its West Side Courthouse! I was the father of the bills that provided for all these;

yet, because I supported the Remsen and Spuyten Duyvil bills, some people have questioned my honest motives. If that's the case, how can you expect legislators to fare who are not the fathers of the parks, the Washington Bridge, the Speedway and the Viaduct?

Now, understand; I ain't defendin' the senators who killed the eighty-cent gas bill. I don't know why they acted as they did; I only want to impress the idea to go slow before you make up your mind that a man, occupyin' the exalted position that I held for so many years, has done wrong. For all I know, these senators may have been as honest and high-minded about the gas bill as I was about the Remsen and Spuyten Duyvil bills.

Plunkitt's Fondest Dream

THE time is comin' and though I'm no youngster, I may see it, when New York City will break away from the State and become a state itself. It's got to come. The feelin' between this city and the hayseeds that make a livin' by plunderin' it is every bit as bitter as the feelin' between the North and South before the war. And, let me tell you, if there ain't a peaceful separation before long, we may have the horrors of civil war right here in New York State. Why, I know a lot of men in my district who would like nothin' better today than to go out gunnin' for hayseeds!

New York City has got a bigger population than most of the states in the Union. It's got more wealth than any dozen of them. Yet the people here, as I explained before, are nothin' but slaves of the Albany gang. We have stood the slavery a long, long time, but the uprisin' is near at hand. It will be a fight for liberty, just like the American Revolution. We'll get liberty peacefully if we can; by cruel war if we must.

Just think how lovely things would be here if we had a Tammany Governor and Legislature meetin', say in the neighborhood of Fifty-ninth Street, and a Tammany Mayor and Board of Aldermen doin' business in City Hall! How sweet and peaceful everything would go on! The people wouldn't have to bother about nothin'. Tammany would take care of everything for them in its nice quiet way. You wouldn't hear of any conflicts between the state and city authorities. They would settle everything pleasant and comfortable at Tammany Hall, and every bill introduced in the Legislature by Tammany would be sure to go through. The Republicans wouldn't count.

Imagine how the city would be built up in a short time! At present we can't make a public improvement of any consequence without goin' to Albany for permission, and most of the time we get turned down when we go there. But, with a Tammany Governor and Legislature up at Fifty-ninth Street, how public works would hum here! The Mayor and Aldermen could decide on an improvement, telephone the Capitol, have a bill put through in a jiffy and—there you are. We could have a state constitution, too, which would extend the debt limit so that we could issue a whole lot more bonds. As things are now, all the money spent for docks, for instance, is charged against the city in calculatin' the debt limit, although the Dock Department provides immense revenues. It's the same with some other departments. This humbug would be dropped if Tammany ruled at the Capitol and the City Hall, and the city would have money to burn.

Another thing—the constitution of the new state wouldn't have a word about civil service, and if any man dared to introduce any kind of a civil service bill in the Legislature, he would be fired out the window. Then we would have government of the people by the people who were elected to govern them. That's the kind of government Lincoln meant. O what a glorious future for the city! Whenever I think of it I feel like goin' out and celebratin', and I'm really almost sorry that I don't drink.

You may ask what would become of the upstate people if New York City left them in the lurch and went into the State business on its own account. Well, we wouldn't be under no obligation to provide for

them; still I would be in favor of helpin' them along
for a while until they could learn to work and earn
an honest livin', just like the United States Government looks after the Indians. These hayseeds have
been so used to livin' off of New York City that they
would be helpless after we left them. It wouldn't do
to let them starve. We might make some sort of an
appropriation for them for a few years, but it would
be with the distinct understandin' that they must get
busy right away and learn to support themselves. If,
after say five years, they weren't self-supportin', we
could withdraw the appropriation and let them shift
for themselves. The plan might succeed and it might
not. We'd be doin' our duty anyhow.

Some persons might say: "But how about it if the
hayseed politicians moved down here and went in to
get control of the government of the new state?" We
could provide against that easy by passin' a law that
these politicians couldn't come below the Bronx without a sort of passport limitin' the time of their stay
here, and forbiddin' them to monkey with politics
here. I don't know just what kind of a bill would be
required to fix this, but with a Tammany Constitution,
Governor, Legislature and Mayor, there would be no
trouble in settlin' a little matter of that sort.

Say, I don't wish I was a poet, for if I was, I guess
I'd be livin' in a garret on no dollars a week instead of
runnin' a great contractin' and transportation business
which is doin' pretty well, thank you; but, honest, now,
the notion takes me sometimes to yell poetry of the
red-hot-hail-glorious-land kind when I think of New
York City as a state by itself.

Tammany's Patriotism

TAMMANY'S the most patriotic organization on earth, notwithstandin' the fact that the civil service law is sappin' the foundations of patriotism all over the country. Nobody pays any attention to the Fourth of July any longer except Tammany and the small boy. When the Fourth comes, the reformers, with Revolutionary names parted in the middle, run off to Newport or the Adirondacks to get out of the way of the noise and everything that reminds them of the glorious day. How different it is with Tammany! The very constitution of the Tammany Society requires that we must assemble at the wigwam on the Fourth, regardless of the weather, and listen to the readin' of the Declaration of Independence and patriotic speeches.

You ought to attend one of these meetin's. They're a liberal education in patriotism. The great hall upstairs is filled with five thousand people, suffocatin' from heat and smoke. Every man Jack of these five thousand knows that down in the basement there's a hundred cases of champagne and two hundred kegs of beer ready to flow when the signal is given. Yet that crowd stick to their seats without turnin' a hair while, for four solid hours, the Declaration of Independence is read, long-winded orators speak, and the glee club sings itself hoarse.

Talk about heroism in the battlefield! That comes

and passes away in a moment. You ain't got time to be anything but heroic. But just think of five thousand men sittin' in the hottest place on earth for four long hours, with parched lips and gnawin' stomachs, and knowin' all the time that the delights of the oasis in the desert were only two flights downstairs! Ah, that is the highest kind of patriotism, the patriotism of long sufferin' and endurance. What man wouldn't rather face a cannon for a minute or two than thirst for four hours, with champagne and beer almost under his nose?

And then see how they applaud and yell when patriotic things are said! As soon as the man on the platform starts off with "when, in the course of human events," word goes around that it's the Declaration of Independence, and a mighty roar goes up. The Declaration ain't a very short document and the crowd has heard it on every Fourth but they give it just as fine a send-off as if it was brand-new and awful excitin'. Then the "long talkers" get in their work, that is two or three orators who are good for an hour each. Heat never has any effect on these men. They use every minute of their time. Sometimes human nature gets the better of a man in the audience and he begins to nod, but he always wakes up with a hurrah for the Declaration of Independence.

The greatest hero of the occasion is the Grand Sachem of the Tammany Society who presides. He and the rest of us Sachems come on the stage wearin' stovepipe hats, accordin' to the constitution, but we can shed ours right off, while the Grand Sachem is required to wear his hat all through the celebration. Have you any idea what that means? Four hours under a big silk hat in a hall where the heat registers 110 and the smoke 250! And the Grand Sachem is expected to look pleasant all the time and say nice things when introducin' the speakers! Often his hand goes to his hat, unconscious-like, then he catches him-self up in time and looks around like a man who is in the tenth story of a burnin' buildin' seekin' a way to escape. I believe that Fourth-of-July silk hat shortened the life of one of our Grand Sachems, the late Supreme Court Justice Smyth, and I know that one of our Sachems refused the office of Grand Sachem because he couldn't get up sufficient patriotism to perform this four-hour hat act. You see, there's degrees of patriotism just as there's degrees in everything else.

You don't hear of the Citizens' Union people holdin' Fourth-of-July celebrations under a five-pound silk hat, or any other way, do you? The Cits take the Fourth like a dog I had when I was a boy. That dog knew as much as some Cits and he acted just like them about the glorious day. Exactly forty-eight hours before each Fourth of July, the dog left our house on a run and hid himself in the Bronx woods. The day after the Fourth he turned up at home as regular as clockwork. He must have known what a dog is up against on the Fourth. Anyhow, he kept out of the way. The name-parted-in-the-middle aristocrats act in just the same way. They don't want to be annoyed with firecrackers and the Declaration of Independence, and when they see the Fourth comin' they hustle off to the woods like my dog.

Tammany don't only show its patriotism at Fourth-of-July celebrations. It's always on deck when the country needs its services. After the Spanish-American War broke out, John J. Scannell, the Tammany leader of the Twenty-fifth District, wrote to Governor Black offerin' to raise a Tammany regiment to go to the front. If you want proof, go to Tammany Hall and see the beautiful set of engrossed resolutions about this regiment. It's true that the Governor didn't accept the offer, but it showed Tammany's patriotism. Some enemies of the organization have said that the offer to raise the regiment was made after the Governor let it be known that no more volunteers were wanted, but that's the talk of envious slanderers.

Now, a word about Tammany's love for the American flag. Did you ever see Tammany Hall decorated for a celebration? It's just a mass of flags. They even take down the window shades and put flags in place of them. There's flags everywhere except on the floors. We don't care for expense where the American flag is concerned, especially after we have won an election. In 1904 we originated the custom of givin' a small flag to each man as he entered Tammany Hall for the Fourth-of-July celebration. It took like wildfire. The men waved their flags whenever they cheered and the sight made me feel so patriotic that I forgot all about civil service for a while. And the good work of the flags didn't stop there. The men carried them home and gave them to the children, and the kids got patriotic, too. Of course, it all cost a pretty penny, but what of that? We had won at the polls the precedin' November, had the offices and could afford to make an extra investment in patriotism.

On the Use of
Money in Politics

THE civil service gang is always howlin' about candidates and officeholders puttin' up money for campaigns and about corporations chippin' in. They might as well howl about givin' contributions to churches. A political organization has to have money for its business as well as a church, and who has more right to put up than the men who get the good things that are goin'? Take, for instance, a great political concern like Tammany Hall. It does missionary work like a church, it's got big expenses and it's got to be supported by the faithful. If a corporation sends in a check to help the good work of the Tammany Society, why shouldn't we take it like other missionary societies? Of course, the day may come when we'll reject the money of the rich as tainted, but it hadn't come when I left Tammany Hall at 11:25 A.M. today.

Not long ago some newspapers had fits because the Assemblyman from my district said he had put up $500 when he was nominated for the Assembly last year. Every politician in town laughed at these papers. I don't think there was even a Citizens' Union man who didn't know that candidates of both parties have to chip in for campaign expenses. The sums they pay are accordin' to their salaries and the length of their terms of office, if elected. Even candidates for the Supreme Court have to fall in line. A Supreme Court Judge in New York County gets $17,500 a year, and he's expected, when nominated, to help along the good cause with a year's salary. Why not? He has fourteen years on the bench ahead of him, and ten thousand other lawyers would be willin' to put up twice as much to be in his shoes. Now, I ain't sayin' that we sell nominations. That's a different thing altogether. There's no auction and no regular biddin'. The man is picked out and somehow he gets to understand what's expected of him in the way of a contribution, and he ponies up—all from gratitude to the organization that honored him, see?

Let me tell you an instance that shows the difference between sellin' nominations and arrangin' them in the way I described. A few years ago a Republican district leader controlled the nomination for Congress in his Congressional district. Four men wanted it. At first the leader asked for bids privately, but decided at last that the best thing to do was to get the four men together in the back room of a certain saloon and have an open auction. When he had his men lined up, he got on a chair, told about the value of the goods for sale, and asked for bids in regular auctioneer style. The highest bidder got the nomination for $5000. Now, that wasn't right at all. These things ought to be always fixed up nice and quiet.

As to officeholders, they would be ingrates if they didn't contribute to the organization that put them in office. They needn't be assessed. That would be against the law. But they know what's expected of them, and if they happen to forget they can be reminded polite and courteous. Dan Donegan, who used to be the Wiskinkie of the Tammany Society, and received contributions from grateful officeholders, had a pleasant way of remindin'. If a man forgot his duty to the organization that made him, Dan would call on the man, smile as sweet as you please and say: "You haven't been round at the Hall lately, have you?" If the man tried to slide around the question, Dan would

say: "It's gettin' awful cold." Then he would have a
fit of shiverin' and walk away. What could be more
polite and, at the same time, more to the point? No
force, no threats—only a little shiverin' which any man
is liable to even in summer.

Just here, I want to charge one more crime to the
infamous civil service law. It has made men turn un-
grateful. A dozen years ago, when there wasn't much
civil service business in the city government, and when
the administration could turn out almost any man
holdin' office, Dan's shiver took effect every time and
there was no ingratitude in the city departments. But
when the civil service law came in and all the clerks
got lead-pipe cinches on their jobs, ingratitude spread
right away. Dan shivered and shook till his bones rat-
tled, but many of the city employees only laughed at
him. One day, I remember, he tackled a clerk in the
Public Works Department, who used to give up pretty
regular, and, after the usual question, began to shiver.
The clerk smiled. Dan shook till his hat fell off. The
clerk took ten cents out of his pocket, handed it to
Dan and said: "Poor man! Go and get a drink to warm
yourself up." Wasn't that shameful? And yet, if it
hadn't been for the civil service law, that clerk would
be contributin' right along to this day.

The civil service law don't cover everything, however. There's lots of good jobs outside its clutch, and
the men that get them are grateful every time. I'm not
speakin' of Tammany Hall alone, remember! It's the
same with the Republican Federal and State officeholders, and every organization that has or has had
jobs to give out—except, of course, the Citizens'
Union. The Cits held office only a couple of years
and, knowin' that they would never be in again, each
Cit officeholder held on for dear life to every dollar
that came his way.

Some people say they can't understand what becomes of all the money that's collected for campaigns.

They would understand fast enough if they were district leaders. There's never been half enough money to go around. Besides the expenses for meetin's, bands and all that, there's the bigger bill for the district workers who get men to the polls. These workers are mostly men who want to serve their country but can't get jobs in the city departments on account of the civil service law. They do the next best thing by keepin' track of the voters and seein' that they come to the polls and vote the right way. Some of these deservin' citizens have to make enough on registration and election days to keep them the rest of the year. Isn't it right that they should get a share of the campaign money?

Just remember that there's thirty-five Assembly districts in New York County, and thirty-six district leaders reachin' out for the Tammany dough-bag for somethin' to keep up the patriotism of ten thousand workers, and you wouldn't wonder that the cry for more, more, is goin' up from every district organization now and forevermore. Amen.

The Successful Politician Does Not Drink

I HAVE explained how to succeed in politics. I want to add that no matter how well you learn to play the political game, you won't make a lastin' success of it if you're a drinkin' man. I never take a drop of any kind of intoxicatin' liquor. I ain't no fanatic. Some of the saloonkeepers are my best friends, and I don't mind goin' into a saloon any day with my friends. But as a matter of business I leave whisky and beer and the rest of that stuff alone. As a matter of business, too, I take for my lieutenants in my district men who don't drink. I tried the other kind for several years, but it didn't pay. They cost too much. For instance, I had a young man who was one of the best hustlers in town. He knew every man in the district, was popular everywhere and could induce a half-dead man to come to the polls on election day. But, regularly, two weeks before election, he started on a drunk, and I had to hire two men to guard him day and night and keep him sober enough to do his work. That cost a lot of money, and I dropped the young man after a while.

Maybe you think I'm unpopular with the saloonkeepers because I don't drink. You're wrong. The most successful saloonkeepers don't drink themselves and they understand that my temperance is a business proposition, just like their own. I have a saloon under my headquarters. If a saloonkeeper gets into trouble, he always knows that Senator Plunkitt is the man to help him out. If there is a bill in the Legislature makin' it easier for the liquor dealers, I am for it every time. I'm one of the best friends the saloon men have—but I don't drink their whisky. I won't go through the temperance lecture dodge and tell you how many bright young men I've seen fall victims to intemperance, but I'll tell you that I could name dozens—young men who had started on the road to statesmanship, who could carry their districts every time, and who could turn out any vote you wanted at the primaries. I honestly believe that drink is the greatest curse of the day, except, of course, civil service, and that it has driven more young men to ruin than anything except civil service examinations.

Look at the great leaders of Tammany Hall! No regular drinkers among them. Richard Croker's strongest drink was vichy. Charlie Murphy takes a glass of wine at dinner sometimes, but he don't go beyond that. A drinkin' man wouldn't last two weeks as leader of Tammany Hall. Nor can a man manage an assembly district long if he drinks. He's got to have a clear head all the time. I could name ten men who, in the last few years, lost their grip in their districts because they began drinkin'. There's now thirty-six district leaders in Tammany Hall, and I don't believe a half-dozen of them ever drink anything except at meals. People have got an idea that because the liquor men are with us in campaigns, our district leaders spend most of their time leanin' against bars. There couldn't be a wronger idea. The district leader makes a business of politics, gets his livin' out of it, and, in order to succeed, he's got to keep sober just like in any other business.

Just take as examples "Big Tim" and "Little Tim" Sullivan. They're known all over the country as the Bowery leaders and, as there's nothin' but saloons on the Bowery, people might think that they are hard drinkers. The fact is that neither of them has ever touched a drop of liquor in his life or even smoked a cigar. Still they don't make no pretenses of being better than anybody else, and don't go around deliverin' temperance lectures. Big Tim made money out of liquor—sellin' it to other people. That's the only way to get good out of liquor.

Look at all the Tammany heads of city departments! There's not a real drinkin' man in the lot. Oh, yes, there are some prominent men in the organization who drink sometimes, but they are not the men who have power. They're ornaments, fancy speakers and all that, who make a fine show behind the footlights, but ain't in it when it comes to directin' the city government and the Tammany organization. The men who sit in the executive committee room at Tammany Hall and direct things are men who celebrate on apollinaris or vichy. Let me tell you what I saw on election night in 1897, when the Tammany ticket swept the city: Up to 10 P.M. Croker, John F. Carroll, Tim Sullivan, Charlie Murphy, and myself sat in the committee room receivin' returns. When nearly all the city was heard from and we saw that Van Wyck was elected by a big majority, I invited the crowd to go across the street for a little celebration. A lot of small politicians followed us, expectin' to see magnums of champagne opened. The waiters in the restaurant expected it, too, and you never saw a more disgusted lot of waiters when they got our orders. Here's the orders: Croker, vichy and bicarbonate of soda; Carroll, seltzer lemonade; Sullivan, apollinaris; Murphy, vichy; Plunkitt, ditto. Before midnight we were all in bed, and next mornin' we were up bright and early attendin' to business, while other men were nursin' swelled heads. Is there anything the matter with temperance as a pure business proposition?

Bosses Preserve
the Nation

WHEN I retired from the Senate, I thought I would take a good, long rest, such a rest as a man needs who has held office for about forty years, and has held four different offices in one year and drawn salaries from three of them at the same time. Drawin' so many salaries is rather fatiguin', you know, and, as I said, I started out for a rest; but when I seen how things were goin' in New York State, and how a great big black shadow hung over us, I said to myself: "No rest for you, George. Your work ain't done. Your country still needs you and you mustn't lay down yet."

What was the great big black shadow? It was the primary election law, amended so as to knock out what are called the party bosses by lettin' in everybody at the primaries and givin' control over them to state officials. Oh, yes, that is a good way to do up the so-called bosses, but have you ever thought what would become of the country if the bosses were put out of business, and their places were taken by a lot of cart-tail orators and college graduates? It would mean chaos. It would be just like takin' a lot of dry-goods clerks and settin' them to run express trains on the New York Central Railroad. It makes my heart bleed to think of it. Ignorant people are always talkin' against party bosses, but just wait till the bosses are gone! Then, and not until then, will they get the right sort of epitaphs, as Patrick Henry or Robert Emmet said.

Look at the bosses of Tammany Hall in the last twenty years. What magnificent men! To them New York City owes pretty much all it is today. John Kelly, Richard Croker, and Charles F. Murphy—what names in American history compare with them, except Washington and Lincoln? They built up the grand Tammany organization, and the organization built up New York. Suppose the city had to depend for the last twenty years on irresponsible concerns like the Citizens' Union, where would it be now? You can make a pretty good guess if you recall the Strong and Low administrations when there was no boss, and the heads of departments were at odds all the time with each other, and the Mayor was at odds with the lot of them. They spent so much time in arguin' and makin' grandstand play, that the interests of the city were forgotten. Another administration of that kind would put New York back a quarter of a century.

Then see how beautiful a Tammany city government runs, with a so-called boss directin' the whole shootin' match! The machinery moves so noiseless that you wouldn't think there was any. If there's any differences of opinion, the Tammany leader settles them quietly, and his orders go every time. How nice it is for the people to feel that they can get up in the mornin' without bein' afraid of seein' in the papers that the Commissioner of Water Supply has sandbagged the Dock Commissioner, and that the Mayor and heads of the departments have been taken to the police court as witnesses! That's no joke. I remember that, under Strong, some commissioners came very near sandbaggin' one another.

Of course, the newspapers like the reform administration. Why? Because these administrations, with their daily rows, furnish as racy news as prizefights or divorce cases. Tammany don't care to get in the pa-

pers. It goes right along attendin' to business quietly
and only wants to be let alone. That's one reason why
the papers are against us.

Some papers complain that the bosses get rich while
devotin' their lives to the interests of the city. What
of it? If opportunities for turnin' an honest dollar
come their way, why shouldn't they take advantage of
them, just as I have done? As I said, in another talk,
there is honest graft and dishonest graft. The bosses
go in for the former. There is so much of it in this
big town that they would be fools to go in for dishonest graft.

Now, the primary election law threatens to do away
with the boss and make the city government a menag-
erie. That's why I can't take the rest I counted on.
I'm goin' to propose a bill for the next session of the
legislature repealin' this dangerous law, and leavin'
the primaries entirely to the organizations themselves,
as they used to be. Then will return the good old
times, when our district leaders could have nice comfortable primary elections at some place selected by
themselves and let in only men that they approved
of as good Democrats. Who is a better judge of the
Democracy of a man who offers his vote than the
leader of the district? Who is better equipped to keep
out undesirable voters?

The men who put through the primary law are the
same crowd that stand for the civil service blight and
they have the same objects in view—the destruction
of governments by party, the downfall of the constitution and hell generally.

Concerning Excise

ALTHOUGH I'm not a drinkin' man myself, I mourn with the poor liquor dealers of New York City, who are taxed and oppressed for the benefit of the farmers up the state. The Raines liquor law is infamous. It takes away nearly all the profits of the saloonkeepers, and then turns in a large part of the money to the State treasury to relieve the hayseeds from taxes. Ah, who knows how many honest, hard-workin' saloonkeepers have been driven to untimely graves by this law! I know personally of a half-dozen who committed suicide because they couldn't pay the enormous license fee, and I have heard of many others. Every time there is an increase of the fee, there is an increase in the suicide record of the city. Now, some of these Republican hayseeds are talkin' about makin' the liquor tax $1500, or even $2000 a year. That would mean the suicide of half of the liquor dealers in the city.

Just see how these poor fellows are oppressed all around! First, liquor is taxed in the hands of the manufacturer by the United States Government; second, the wholesale dealer pays a special tax to the government; third, the retail dealer is specially taxed by the United States Government; fourth, the retail dealer has to pay a big tax to the State government.

Now, liquor dealing is criminal or it ain't. If it's

criminal, the men engaged in it ought to be sent to prison. If it ain't criminal, they ought to be protected and encouraged to make all the profit they honestly can. If it's right to tax a saloonkeeper $1000, it's right to put a heavy tax on dealers in other beverages—in milk, for instance—and make the dairymen pay up. But what a howl would be raised if a bill was introduced in Albany to compel the farmers to help support the State government! What would be said of a law that put a tax of, say $60 on a grocer, $150 on a dry-goods man, and $500 more if he includes the other goods that are kept in a country store?

If the Raines law gave the money extorted from the saloonkeepers to the city, there might be some excuse for the tax. We would get some benefit from it, but it gives a big part of the tax to local option localities where the people are always shoutin' that liquor dealin' is immoral. Ought these good people be subjected to the immoral influence of money taken from the saloons—tainted money? Out of respect for the tender consciences of these pious people, the Raines law ought to exempt them from all contamination from the plunder that comes from the saloon traffic. Say, mark that sarcastic. Some people who ain't used to fine sarcasm might think I meant it.

The Raines people make a pretense that the high license fee promotes temperance. It's just the other way around. It makes more intemperance and, what is as bad, it makes a monopoly in dram-shops. Soon the saloons will be in the hands of a vast trust, and any stuff can be sold for whisky or beer. It's gettin' that way already. Some of the poor liquor dealers in my district have been forced to sell wood alcohol for whisky, and many deaths have followed. A half-dozen men died in a couple of days from this kind of whisky which was forced down their throats by the high liquor tax. If they raise the tax higher, wood alcohol will be too costly, and I guess some dealers will have to get down to kerosene oil and add to the Rockefeller millions.

The way the Raines law divides the different classes of licenses is also an outrage. The sumptuous hotel saloons, with $10,000 paintin's and bricky-brac and Oriental splendors gets off easier than a shanty on the rocks, by the water's edge in my district where boatmen drink their grog, and the only ornaments is a three-cornered mirror nailed to the wall, and a chromo of the fight between Tom Hyer and Yankee Sullivan. Besides, a premium is put on places that sell liquor not to be drunk on the premises, but to be taken home. Now, I want to declare that from my experience in New York City, I would rather see rum sold in the dram-shops unlicensed, provided the rum is swallowed on the spot, than to encourage, by a low tax, "bucket-shops" from which the stuff is carried into the tenements at all hours of the day and night and make drunkenness and debauchery among the women and children. A "bucket-shop" in the tenement district means a cheap, so-called distillery, where raw spirits, poisonous colorin' matter and water are sold for brandy and whisky at ten cents a quart, and carried away in buckets and pitchers; I have always noticed that there are many undertakers wherever the "bucket-shop" flourishes, and they have no dull seasons.

I want it understood that I'm not an advocate of the liquor dealers or of drinkin'. I think every man would be better off if he didn't take any intoxicatin' drink at all, but as men will drink, they ought to have good stuff without impoverishin' themselves by goin' to fancy places and without riskin' death by goin' to poor places. The State should look after their interests as well as the interests of those who drink nothin' stronger than milk.

Now, as to the liquor dealers themselves. They ain't the criminals that cantin' hypocrites say they are. I know lots of them and I know that, as a rule, they're good honest citizens who conduct their business in a straight, honorable way. At a convention of the liquor dealers a few years ago, a big city official welcomed them on behalf of the city and said: "Go on elevatin' your standard higher and higher. Go on with your good work. Heaven will bless you!" That was puttin' it just a little strong, but the sentiment was all right and I guess the speaker went a bit further than he intended in his enthusiasm over meetin' such a fine set of men and, perhaps, dinin' with them.

A Parting Word on the Future of the Democratic Party in America

THE Democratic party of the nation ain't dead, though it's been givin' a lifelike imitation of a corpse for several years. It can't die while it's got Tammany for its backbone. The trouble is that the party's been chasin' after theories and stayin' up nights readin' books instead of studyin' human nature and actin' accordin', as I've advised in tellin' how to hold your district. In two Presidential campaigns, the leaders talked themselves red in the face about silver bein' the best money and gold bein' no good, and they tried to prove it out of books. Do you think the people cared for all that guff? No. They heartily indorsed what Richard Croker said at the Hoffman House one day in 1900. "What's the use of discussin' what's the best kind of money?" said Croker. "I'm in favor of all kinds of money—the more the better." See how a real Tammany statesman can settle in twenty-five words a problem that monopolized two campaigns!

Then imperialism. The Democratic party spent all its breath on that in the last national campaign. Its position was all right, sure, but you can't get people excited about the Philippines. They've got too much at home to interest them; they're too busy makin' a livin' to bother about the niggers in the Pacific. The party's got to drop all them put-you-to-sleep issues and come out in 1908 for somethin' that will wake the people up; somethin' that will make it worth while to work for the party.

There's just one issue that would set this country on fire. The Democratic party should say in the first plank of its platform: "We hereby declare, in national convention assembled, that the paramount issue now, always and forever, is the abolition of the iniquitous and villainous civil service laws which are destroyin' all patriotism, ruinin' the country and takin' away good jobs from them that earn them. We pledge ourselves, if our ticket is elected, to repeal those laws at once and put every civil service reformer in jail."

Just imagine the wild enthusiasm of the party, if that plank was adopted, and the rush of Republicans to join us in restorin' our country to what it was before this college professor's nightmare, called civil service reform, got hold of it! Of course, it would be all right to work in the platform some stuff about the tariff and sound money and the Philippines, as no platform seems to be complete without them, but they wouldn't count. The people would read only the first plank and then hanker for election day to come to put the Democratic party in office.

I see a vision. I see the civil service monster lyin' flat on the ground. I see the Democratic party standin' over it with a foot on its neck and wearin' the crown of victory. I see Thomas Jefferson lookin' out from a cloud and sayin': "Give him another sockdologer; finish him." And I see millions of men wavin' their hats and singin' "Glory Hallelujah!"

Strenuous Life of the Tammany District Leader

NOTE: *This chapter is based on extracts from Plunkitt's Diary and on my daily observation of the work of the district leader.*—W.L.R.

THE life of the Tammany district leader is strenuous. To his work is due the wonderful recuperative power of the organization.

One year it goes down in defeat and the prediction is made that it will never again raise its head. The district leader, undaunted by defeat, collects his scattered forces, organizes them as only Tammany knows how to organize, and in a little while the organization is as strong as ever.

No other politician in New York or elsewhere is exactly like the Tammany district leader or works as he does. As a rule, he has no business or occupation other than politics. He plays politics every day and night in the year, and his headquarters bears the inscription, "Never closed."

Everybody in the district knows him. Everybody knows where to find him, and nearly everybody goes to him for assistance of one sort or another, especially the poor of the tenements.

He is always obliging. He will go to the police courts to put in a good word for the "drunks and disorderlies" or pay their fines, if a good word is not effective.

He will attend christenings, weddings, and funerals. He will feed the hungry and help bury the dead.

A philanthropist? Not at all. He is playing politics all the time.

Brought up in Tammany Hall, he has learned how to reach the hearts of the great mass of voters. He does not bother about reaching their heads. It is his belief that arguments and campaign literature have never gained votes.

He seeks direct contact with the people, does them good turns when he can, and relies on their not forgetting him on election day. His heart is always in his work, too, for his subsistence depends on its results.

If he holds his district and Tammany is in power, he is amply rewarded by a good office and the opportunities that go with it. What these opportunities are has been shown by the quick rise to wealth of so many Tammany district leaders. With the examples before him of Richard Croker, once leader of the Twentieth District; John F. Carroll, formerly leader of the Twenty-ninth; Timothy ("Dry Dollar") Sullivan, late leader of the Sixth, and many others, he can always look forward to riches and ease while he is going through the drudgery of his daily routine.

This is a record of a day's work by Plunkitt:

2 A.M.: Aroused from sleep by the ringing of his doorbell; went to the door and found a bartender, who asked him to go to the police station and bail out a saloonkeeper who had been arrested for violating the excise law. Furnished bail and returned to bed at three o'clock.

6 A.M.: Awakened by fire engines passing his house. Hastened to the scene of the fire, according to the custom of the Tammany district leaders, to give assistance to the fire sufferers, if needed. Met several of his election district captains who are always under orders to look out for fires, which are considered great vote-getters. Found several tenants who had been burned out,

took them to a hotel, supplied them with clothes, fed them, and arranged temporary quarters for them until they could rent and furnish new apartments.

8:30 A.M.: Went to the police court to look after his constituents. Found six "drunks." Secured the discharge of four by a timely word with the judge, and paid the fines of two.

9 A.M.: Appeared in the Municipal District Court. Directed one of his district captains to act as counsel for a widow against whom dispossess proceedings had been instituted and obtained an extension of time. Paid the rent of a poor family about to be dispossessed and gave them a dollar for food.

11 A.M.: At home again. Found four men waiting for him. One had been discharged by the Metropolitan Railway Company for neglect of duty, and wanted the district leader to fix things. Another wanted a job on the road. The third sought a place on the Subway and the fourth, a plumber, was looking for work with the Consolidated Gas Company. The district leader spent nearly three hours fixing things for the four men, and succeeded in each case.

3 P.M.: Attended the funeral of an Italian as far as the ferry. Hurried back to make his appearance at the funeral of a Hebrew constituent. Went conspicuously to the front both in the Catholic church and the synagogue, and later attended the Hebrew confirmation ceremonies in the synagogue.

7 P.M.: Went to district headquarters and presided over a meeting of election district captains. Each captain submitted a list of all the voters in his district, reported on their attitude toward Tammany, suggested who might be won over and how they could be won, told who were in need, and who were in trouble of any kind and the best way to reach them. District leader took notes and gave orders.

8 P.M.: Went to a church fair. Took chances on everything, bought ice cream for the young girls and the

children. Kissed the little ones, flattered their mothers and took their fathers out for something down at the corner.

9 P.M.: At the clubhouse again. Spent $10 on tickets for a church excursion and promised a subscription for a new church bell. Bought tickets for a baseball game to be played by two nines from his district. Listened to the complaints of a dozen pushcart peddlers who said they were persecuted by the police and assured them he would go to Police Headquarters in the morning and see about it.

10:30 P.M.: Attended a Hebrew wedding reception and dance. Had previously sent a handsome wedding present to the bride.

12 P.M.: In bed.

That is the actual record of one day in the life of Plunkitt. He does some of the same things every day, but his life is not so monotonous as to be wearisome.

Sometimes the work of a district leader is exciting, especially if he happens to have a rival who intends to make a contest for the leadership at the primaries. In that case, he is even more alert, tries to reach the fires before his rival, sends out runners to look for "drunks and disorderlies" at the police stations, and keeps a very close watch on the obituary columns of the newspapers.

A few years ago there was a bitter contest for the Tammany leadership of the Ninth District between John C. Sheehan and Frank J. Goodwin. Both had had long experience in Tammany politics and both understood every move of the game.

Every morning their agents went to their respective headquarters before seven o'clock and read through the death notices in all the morning papers. If they found that anybody in the district had died, they rushed to the homes of their principals with the information and then there was a race to the house of the deceased to offer condolences, and, if the family were poor, something more substantial.

On the day of the funeral there was another contest. Each faction tried to surpass the other in the number and appearance of the carriages it sent to the funeral, and more than once they almost came to blows at the church or in the cemetery.

On one occasion the Goodwinites played a trick on their adversaries which has since been imitated in other districts. A well-known liquor dealer who had a considerable following died, and both Sheehan and Goodwin were eager to become his political heir by making a big showing at the funeral.

Goodwin managed to catch the enemy napping. He went to all the livery stables in the district, hired all the carriages for the day, and gave orders to two hundred of his men to be on hand as mourners.

Sheehan had never had any trouble about getting all the carriages that he wanted, so he let the matter go until the night before the funeral. Then he found that he could not hire a carriage in the district.

He called his district committee together in a hurry and explained the situation to them. He could get all the vehicles he needed in the adjoining district, he said, but if he did that, Goodwin would rouse the voters of the Ninth by declaring that he (Sheehan) had patronized foreign industries.

Finally, it was decided that there was nothing to do but to go over to Sixth Avenue and Broadway for carriages. Sheehan made a fine turnout at the funeral, but the deceased was hardly in his grave before Goodwin raised the cry of "Protection to home industries," and denounced his rival for patronizing livery-stable keepers outside of his district. The cry had its effect in the primary campaign. At all events, Goodwin was elected leader.

A recent contest for the leadership of the Second

District illustrated further the strenuous work of the Tammany district leaders. The contestants were Patrick Divver, who had managed the district for years, and Thomas F. Foley.

Both were particularly anxious to secure the large Italian vote. They not only attended all the Italian christenings and funerals, but also kept a close lookout for the marriages in order to be on hand with wedding presents.

At first, each had his own reporter in the Italian quarter to keep track of the marriages. Later, Foley conceived a better plan. He hired a man to stay all day at the City Hall marriage bureau, where most Italian couples go through the civil ceremony, and telephone to him at his saloon when anything was doing at the bureau.

Foley had a number of presents ready for use and, whenever he received a telephone message from his man, he hastened to the City Hall with a ring or a watch or a piece of silver and handed it to the bride with his congratulations. As a consequence, when Divver got the news and went to the home of the couple with his present, he always found that Foley had been ahead of him. Toward the end of the campaign, Divver also stationed a man at the marriage bureau and then there were daily foot races and fights between the two heelers.

Sometimes the rivals came into conflict at the deathbed. One night a poor Italian peddler died in Roosevelt Street. The news reached Divver and Foley about the same time, and as they knew the family of the man was destitute, each went to an undertaker and brought him to the Roosevelt Street tenement.

The rivals and the undertakers met at the house and an altercation ensued. After much discussion the Divver undertaker was selected. Foley had more carriages at the funeral, however, and he further impressed the Italian voters by paying the widow's rent for a month, and sending her half a ton of coal and a barrel of flour.

The rivals were put on their mettle toward the end of the campaign by the wedding of a daughter of one of the original Cohens of the Baxter Street region. The Hebrew vote in the district is nearly as large as the Italian vote, and Divver and Foley set out to capture the Cohens and their friends.

They stayed up nights thinking what they would give the bride. Neither knew how much the other was prepared to spend on a wedding present, or what form it would take; so spies were employed by both sides to keep watch on the jewelry stores, and the jewelers of the district were bribed by each side to impart the desired information.

At last Foley heard that Divver had purchased a set of silver knives, forks and spoons. He at once bought a duplicate set and added a silver tea service. When the presents were displayed at the home of the bride, Divver was not in a pleasant mood and he charged his jeweler with treachery. It may be added that Foley won at the primaries.

One of the fixed duties of a Tammany district leader is to give two outings every summer, one for the men of his district and the other for the women and children, and a beefsteak dinner and a ball every winter. The scene of the outings is, usually, one of the groves along the Sound.

The ambition of the district leader on these occasions is to demonstrate that his men have broken all records in the matter of eating and drinking. He gives out the exact number of pounds of beef, poultry, butter, etc., that they have consumed and professes to know how many potatoes and ears of corn have been served.

According to his figures, the average eating record of each man at the outing is about ten pounds of beef, two or three chickens, a pound of butter, a half peck of potatoes, and two dozen ears of corn. The drinking records, as given out, are still more phenomenal. For some reason, not yet explained, the district leader thinks that his popularity will be greatly increased if he can show that his followers can eat and drink more than the followers of any other district leader.

The same idea governs the beefsteak dinners in the winter. It matters not what sort of steak is served or how it is cooked; the district leader considers only the question of quantity, and when he excels all others in this particular, he feels, somehow, that he is a bigger man and deserves more patronage than his associates in the Tammany Executive Committee.

As to the balls, they are the events of the winter in the extreme East Side and West Side society. Mamie and Maggie and Jennie prepare for them months in advance, and their young men save up for the occasion just as they save for the summer trips to Coney Island.

The district leader is in his glory at the opening of the ball. He leads the cotillion with the prettiest woman present—his wife, if he has one, permitting—and spends almost the whole night shaking hands with his constituents. The ball costs him a pretty penny, but he has found that the investment pays.

By these means the Tammany district leader reaches out into the homes of his district, keeps watch not only on the men, but also on the women and children; knows their needs, their likes and dislikes, their troubles and their hopes, and places himself in a position to use his knowledge for the benefit of his organization and himself. Is it any wonder that scandals do not permanently disable Tammany and that it speedily recovers from what seems to be crushing defeat?

WRITINGS FROM THE AMERICAN BODY POLITIC

THE FEDERALIST PAPERS *Alexander Hamilton, James Madison & John Jay*

628810

Edited by Clinton Rossiter, with an introduction and notes by Charles R. Kesler

These are some of the most fundamental writings of the American political landscape. Here are the thoughts of the architects of the strong, united government that we have today. This collection contains all eighty-five papers from the edition first published in 1788. It also includes the complete *Constitution*, with marginal notes for relevant passages of the text.

THE ANTI-FEDERALIST PAPERS & *the Constitutional Convention Debates*

edited by Ralph Hetchem

52884-0

While the Federalists supported a strong central government, the Anti-Federalists saw this as a threat to personal freedom and the liberties so hard-won from England. This split, between the desire for local control and the idea of a centralized power, is one of the major causes of the Civil War.

THE CONSTITUTION OF THE UNITED STATES

An Introduction *Floyd G. Cullop*

627245

The *Constitution* is among the world's most remarkable political documents. Yet, far too few Americans know anything about it. This book, which clearly explains our *Constitution*, is a "must" for every American.

Available wherever books are sold or at signetclassics.com

AMERICAN VOICES

THE JUNGLE by Upton Sinclair 528042

In writing some of the most harrowing scenes ever in modern literature, Upton Sinclair vividly depicted factory life in Chicago in the first years of the 20th century.

LIFE ON THE MISSISSIPPI by Mark Twain 528174

At once a romantic history of a mighty river, an autobiographical account of Twain's early steamboat days, and a storehouse of humorous anecdotes and sketches, it is an epochal record of America's vanished past that earned for its author his first recognition as a serious writer.

O PIONEERS! by Willa Cather 522850

The author's second novel, in which she creates the first of her memorable heroines. Alexandra Bergson inherits her father's failing farm, raises her brothers alone, and is torn by the emergence of an unexpected passion.

THE SONG OF THE LARK by Willa Cather 525337

Thea Kronberg is a feisty girl whose upbringing in a raw, provincial Colorado town nearly stifles her artistic ambitions. Here is a wonderful portrait of a young woman who makes her own destiny.

WINESBURG, OHIO by Sherwood Anderson 529952

Combines Sherwood Anderson's memories of his boyhood in Clyde, Ohio, and his observations in turn-of-the-century Chicago. A modern American classic that embraces frankness and truth, and deals with people whose deeply moving lives are filled with secrets.

AMERICAN CLASSICS

SPOON RIVER ANTHOLOGY by *Edgar Lee Masters*
with an Introduction by John Hollander
A book of dramatic monologues written in free verse about a fictional
town called Spoon River, based on the Midwestern towns where
Edgar Lee Masters grew up.
0-451-52530-2

SELECTED WRITINGS OF RALPH WALDO EMERSON
with an Introduction by Charles Johnson
Fourteen essays and addresses including *The Oversoul, Politics,
Thoreau, Divinity School Address,* as well as poems *Threnody* and
Uriel, and selections from his letters and journals. Includes Chronology
and Bibliography.
0-451-52907-3

EVANGELINE & Selected Tales and Poems
by Henry Wadsworth Longfellow
Edited by Horace Gregory, with a new introduction by Edward Cifelli
Includes *The Witnesses, The Courtship of Miles Standish,* and
selections from *Hiawatha,* with commentaries on Longfellow by Van
Wyck Brooks, Norman Holmes Pearson, and Lewis Carroll. Includes
Introduction, Bibliography, and Chronology.
0-451-52003-3

WALDEN AND CIVIL DISOBEDIENCE by *Henry David Thoreau*
150th Anniversary Edition
Two classic examinations of individuality in relation to nature, society,
and government. *Walden* conveys at once a naturalist's wonder at the
commonplace and a Transcendentalist's yearning for spiritual truth. "Civil
Disobedience," perhaps the most famous essay in American literature,
has inspired activists like Martin Luther King, Jr. and Gandhi.
0-451-52945-6

Available wherever books are sold or at
signetclassics.com

Read more about the Early American Experience

THE AUTOBIOGRAPHY & Other Writings
Benjamin Franklin
528107
THE AUTOBIOGRAPHY provides an important insight into the mind of one of the founders of American democracy. This volume also includes *The Way to Wealth, Essays to Do Good*, selections from his scientific and political work, and writings on family, life, and religion.

THE LAST OF THE MOHICANS
James Fenimore Cooper
527658
Moving with the speed of a classic Western, this story tells of the adventures of Natty Bumppo and Chingachgook as they travel through hostile territory in Canada and Upstate New York during the French and Indian War.

THE LEGEND OF SLEEPY HOLLOW
& OTHER STORIES IN THE SKETCH BOOK
Washington Irving
524950
Sage, storyteller, wit and keen observer of the American scene, Irving has been called, "the first ambassador the new world of letters has sent to the old." These well-known tales have continued to delight and entertain readers many years after they were first written.

Available wherever books are sold or at signetclassics.com

READ THE TOP 20 SIGNET CLASSICS

SIGNETCLASSICS.COM